AF444463

LETTERS OF HERESY:

Uncovering the Skies

Shining in Red

A Novel By

Stemarcus

Translation From Macedonian: Stemarcus

Proofreading: Marija Petkovska

"Knowing oneself is the beginning of all wisdom."

Aristotle

PROLOGUE

Standing in the middle of the regular hexagon, he was completely absorbed.

His breathing, much like the enveloping darkness, was already losing intensity with every next breath becoming curtailed and shallower.

His feet, slowly, joyously, separated themselves from the stairs made of the noblest material from which he also was once made of. Walking upwards, he was becoming more and more assured that the peak was within reach. The tranquil dance of his eyelids was slowly becoming superfluous, blending them into embrace.

He didn't feel the need to leave the eyes open when witnessing the absolute world of noumena in the way he had been trying to elevate himself into since the days spent in the central cathedral, striving to overflow it into an everyday dream. The peak was here.

No, it wasn't an elation-uplift or some kind of numinous transience covered by the abstract art of the moment.

The truth of the ever-more-present world has always been one.. And it was not present neither in life nor in death. The problem is that you can't spot the truth looking upwards from below. You have to be above it, above all other truths and illusions about the world and about yourself. You need to be above all the heavens and to have eyes that penetrate all the clouds, earth mists and dense forests in order to reach the buried treasures.

Beginning from this moment, the eyes were also as redundant as the attempts at rational breakthrough into the essence of the sense unfathomable.

He was finally in possession of wings that carried him higher than any sky, even though he felt no need to motion his head downwards.

He was the very supreme angel to whom God himself had entrusted and promised, during his many previous lives, a Hexagonal Throne, from where he would lay out His wisdom throughout the world in the form of a letter written for those who felt their eyes redundant.

1. Eros

WHEN THE LIGHT BECOMES TOO STRONG

It became indeterminate and unimportant for the artist that evening whether he saw a new path through reality or a divine illusion.

The ecstasy blinded his judgmental abilities to the extent that he did not know whether he felt afraid or was experiencing bliss.

The liquids and scents were perceived so realistically, while offering exalting transcendence.

She was there.

A moment before raising the shroud again, focusing on the empty sight of the closed window, he thought of the final victory over the darkness.

In one single movement he picked up the large canvas cloak and the miraculous sculpture appeared.

They were One.

She couldn't be distinguished from the being of the one who served as a mold for its creation.

The sculpture embodied partial representation of a female face created by three overlapping ouroboroses[1] placed at a right angle.

The careful eye could not fail noticing the simulation of a human sexual act in one of the three.

Her Ego, Super-Ego and Id. Love, Thought and Courage. Light, Darkness and Color.

"Whore! Saint! Equally beautiful in the divine essence!" he addressed her.

The marble sculpture glanced silently somewhere behind him with a pondering gaze.

Her creator was forever out of the sense perceivable.

After a few moments, she began trembling.

From the forehead of the woman that was his madness, obscure shadowy Shapes began emanating with supernatural splendor.

The light got simply too strong. The atelier became the main source of light in the Universe.

It was alternating all visible and invisible colors, but the artist's eyes were able to see the game of cosmic perfections and restore the space-time continuums that contained his memories.

The form was an inextinguishable fire in movement. Pulsating, much like the feelings.

It was gradually dwindling, taking up the increasingly sophisticated, anticipated shape.

Soon it became pure light in movement of the somewhat recognizable figure that emerged from the artistic creation.

"Forget me, tormented one!" she spoke to him, "do you not see that..."

Maximilian Comnenius did not dare touch the creation at a point higher than her legs, believing in the divinity of the creation.

"I am Death! And Death sows nothing but death! No mortal soul is allowed to address me."

"I'm Life!" he replied, "and I have a reason to talk to you."

"No reason known to a wandered mind like yours may be compared with the reason for you to enjoy your own creation. Create. The past only destroys. "

"The most perfect creation of my mind is You."

"You're right. I am a creation, not reality."

"The only reality is the one of the Mind."

"The only reality is the one that could give the mind hope for life. And it could not live in it for long without knowing it. "

The sculptor finally turned his gaze upward, toward what could be called anything but a face.

The light from which it was created spilled from one end to the other.

Once all the light spilled from one of the ends, the facial figure would switched to the other side and return back whence it came from.

"Your face is an hourglass of light," he said approaching closer but the next moment it spilled all across the space.

Innumerable light entities started touching every point of the room.

***

The next day the artist returned to the marble statue with a clearer and sharper mind. As did the light, suddenly appearing and taking for a nuance a clearer shape.

"Why is your face still enveloped in fog?" he asked her.

"It is the fog of your imperfect imagination" she replied, stepping out in a half-circle.

"Katya, I thought you've always been perfectly close to my mind. You are the only and truly authentic name of Passion itself. "

"I shall remain out of reach forever."

Maximilian lowered his gaze and looked down. In the front parts of his face he felt almost frantic circulation of all the pain in the world while the adrenal gland lost its sense of time dancing a tango with his heart.

"But… darn you, loveless woman, we could make a deal that will increase my purity in your eyes!"

His shimmering irises instantly widened.

"You will have to create and dedicate to me six statues that will represent me in six different ways, giving me tangible shape that corresponds each of the six types of Love: Eros, Ludus, Storge, Pragma, Mania and Agape. Eros, as an erotic trance, desire to become one and a long lasting desire of intimate culmination. Ludus, like a young, crazy, surmountable love. First love. Storge, as a friendly, devoted, mature love that's open for help, confession and repentance.

Pragma as an attraction that serves for the benefit of both sides. A generous gift that can help both into climbing the scale of sublimity - the earthly as well as the heavenly one. Mania as an obsession, fanaticism, faith that gives birth to devotion without which no form of sensory and intelligent action could give fruit. Agape, like pure, eternal, godlike love. An immeasurable ocean of unbreakable harmony resulting from the perfect, God-determined fusion of the five previously mentioned rivers.

The right edge of his lips rose along with his abrupt sigh.

"Every next one of them, depending on your refinement and constant upgrading, will either purify or blur me. This means you'll need to learn constantly."

The mixture of animalistic innocence and artistic flow that was drowning him, forced him to nod his head in confirmation.

"Don't forget: each of them belongs to me" she stretched out her palm facing downwards.

The Artist reached out with his own hand and the bright figure spread out its wings across the space, blindingly shining with such a glare for the first time since her emanation.

"Now I am pure divine energy" a voice could be heard through the mists.

The eyes of the artist could recognize a kaleidoscope of memories in the infinity of shapes, and maybe fragments of what was yet to come. The unification of the separate pieces of light undetectably turned his inner being on and off while it swam on tachycardia in a middle of a sea of warmth and cold.

Their crystallization once more disrupted his consciousness for a moment. He shut his eyes firmly and then he opened them again. A map began drawing itself upon the emerald irises, a map of a mind-silenced unsettlement. The beauty was laying in the middle of the spacious table surrounded by bronze and other metals and marble.

"This time I shall be the sculptor of your world" he spoke to her, gradually getting his lips closer to hers until her body completely disappeared.

SCULPTING APPARITIONS IS A DUTY OF PASSION

The sculptor left his home and tried to study the topology of the world during the walk.

It seemed as if the snow cover, was creating another city within Marckest.

The houses were crammed like grain fields. All of them tiny, round shaped, identical in the perfect sharing of the surrounding space. Their borders were marking almost perfect squares.

The buildings were sharp and tall. Unscrupulously breaking the city core in pieces between the richer and the poorer parts. They reminded him of the past.

In the sandwich between buildings and houses, his artistic home, the ghetto, was flattened in.

It was Tuesday, a dreary day in which the basic source of light was the snow.

An unusually animated day.

The increased traffic from all sides was held prisoner by the fog it itself created.

The city's atmosphere and the heavenly grayness were meant to be the perfect neighbors.

After few hours a pale sun arose, changing the feeling that occurs every time you mix with other people.

"Hey Maxim!" a friend's voice could be heard coming from across the street.

The sculptor lifted his head. There were three of them.

"How've you been, soldier! It must've been a hundred years since we saw each other last time. Staying anywhere nearby?" he hugged him.

Maxim, lifting his eyebrows greetingly with a semi-focused glance, turned his head towards the other two in the background.

"Jimmy!" he recalled the once-best friend.

"The man with whom you've been like a camel through the eye of a needle... what's up?"

Maxim smirked.

"I'm headed to the studio. What are you all up to?"

"Pussywipped once again, eh, soldier?" laughed Jimmy. "We're getting ready for a little party tonight. There's this gig at Robbie's place to which you, mister, seem to be invited as a VIP guest. Alongside with, er... Mariana", Jimmy winked.

"Robbie..." he addressed one of his two friends, "meet Maxim. Maxim, this is Robbie. Have a long and lasting love, but please, by all means, do not get caught. This society has a strange custom to treat such love in an overly gay manner."

Jimmy was a thirty-year-old famous guitarist, singer, a Sagittarius, and a well know urban chap. He had an illegitimate son and a band with which he played various types of rock: garage, surf rock, psychedelic, and punk. The Sagittarius. One of the not-so-big bands, yet with steadily growing popularity among adolescents and all sorts of younger audience in the city.

Jimmy was an open-minded extrovert whose thoughts expressed, were, and needed music.

By the age of thirty, he had a high three-digit number of females for occasional friendship and only one serious relationship, with the fruit being a five-year-old Matthew, who, after the sudden death of Jimmy's fiancée, lived with Jimmy's father.

"Let me think about it, I'll give you a call later. In any case, thank you for the invitation."

"Look at him - he would *think about it*. Bro, that *thinking* shit got you the way you are."

"Could be..."

"Soldier, you better show up. Me and the guys will be expecting you there."

"Okay, Mr. Jimmy Hendrix."

Bumping fists in salute, both went their own way.

***

"Katya, my omnipresent truth!" - whispered the poet, seeing the divine illusion of a bare body cutting through the cigarette smoke in a zigzag.

He looked at her with purity incomparable to any before.

The drunk crowd in the cabaret club couldn't see anything. And nothing is more blinding than reality.

The loud music established a monopoly over their attention, hammering out auto hypnotic tools from the earthly passions and urges for aggression.

The sight was a privilege of the one who could sculpt worlds even out of a mist, worlds that are truer than any predominantly subjective game between the senses and the mind, conceived as *truth*.

The almost naked body approached with a speed of thinking for which the mind in such a state was capable of.

The transparent sheet with which it was covered just flew away. Blown away by the wind of the sculptor's eyes which were indefinitely long lost and fixed on a single point.

Soon the only fabric that remained on her body was that of the lingerie, black, mysterious, with the elegance with which only the divine eyes were endowed. In the middle there were drawings-replicas of *The Birth of Venus*. The shape resembled her lips in a miraculous way. Dark purple lipstick. Able to seize all of the attention and reason of the sculptor.

Her lips were a drug with her tongue as the secret ingredient.

Each circular twirl of the tongue through the lips of the sculptor gave birth to a crazed butterfly in his stomach.

The strongest erection in his life gave the sculptor enough energy to rise up and give her his hands, leading her into an irrevocable state.

Holding her by the hand, he hurriedly left the room.

There was a sign on the toilet door - *Out of order.*

It was empty.

He locked the door and, at the same instant, turned her body around, leaning her on the sink.

The skin of her butt was softer than Chinese silk. From her mildly shivering back, cold streams sprang f which the artist, too, could feel. Her legs were trembling excitedly, as of a teenage girl.

He touched her lady parts which were no less wet than the insides of her mouth.

Whole variety of universes built within minuscule drops, getting ready to go through their natural cycles.

Every touch, splendidly gauged on the scale of human pleasure, meant zestful thirst but also, on his part, a restraint to the point that she wanted infinitely many more and more.

Her solar plexus played with the air, taking it in and out in the most natural rhythm directed by him, as if her whole shape represented a musical instrument played by an outstanding virtuoso.

With every segment of her back – the shoulder blades, the teres major, the teres minor, following the deep back line all the way to her lats and ending with her luscious bottom, even her legs, trembling and resonating with the inner rhythm, she felt like belonging to an all-knowing almost-divine being promising to take her whole carnality towards the sky through the senses of pleasure, promising to spiral it upwards uncontrollably with every new contact.

That promise was either torn into pieces or entirely fulfilled when he placed two fingers deep inside, she could not tell at the moment.

The intervals between the instinctive sighs became shorter, as did her patience.

The deluge of passions metamorphosed into mindful touches was continuing its competition with all the other instincts.

He pulled it out and rubbed it. Her every inch was mildly and leniently quivering.

Her nipple-crowned breasts were sharper than the tone she usually used to address him.

Entering the irreversible play of bodily passions, she went down on her knees and placed her specially designed lips in the natural place. Her face became One with the body of the artist.

"That's a really nice lipstick" he said to her.

"I only use it for blowjobs" she replied.

"You know, it is exactly right now that your face is perfect," said the Artist, "and all the time I was wondering what was missing."

The elegance with which the act was performed was part of her unearthly identity.

She knew all the perfect moments: when to move with the bottom lip, when with the upper, when to make circles with her little tongue, when to bite challengingly.

She pulled the phallus towards her, touched her nipples with it and rubbed that manhood all across her face.

"My face belongs to him" she said telepathically, calmly taking it again in her mouth.

Only her mouth and throat were able to fit it all the way.

She put it in and took it out as quickly as possible without the slightest signs of gagging.

Finally, he grabbed her by the hair and lifted her up.

Turning her around, he made her lean her left knee on the toilet.

Slowly, very slowly, he spread her legs until he entered

her.

With several circular movements upon the penetration, the widening reached its peak.

She surely liked it best from behind.

Soon the artist dynamized the pace, moving up and down with ever-more increasing speeds.

His experience enabled him to adapt.

The mild curvature of the organ allowed touching of the G-spot.

Perfection itself was an inevitable temptation with the power to transform aesthetic judgments into pure experiences.

His length and her width were complementary to each other as if out of a fairy tale.

"Katya, this turns out like Plato's Myth... The Lord created us as a puzzle of two pieces and separated us. And we have found ourselves again" he said to her.

"Oh, my dear... I only belong to you, entirely, completely - with body and soul."

By reading her bodily signs, he was determining the speed and direction.

He caught her by her shiny red hair and, covering her mouth, he didn't let her make a sound.

"You make me feel like a real woman" her telepathy echoed once more.

He picked up the pace.

The sink and the toilet that were next to each other began to shake.

Someone tried to enter, knocking on the toilet door that had the sign saying it was out of order.

With a slight change of the pose, Maximilian managed to accelerate even more.

He penetrated radiating with energy. Once more, he had to punish the whore for all the sufferings and restlessness he went through, for all the, goddamn whorish behavior.

She forgot herself in her moaning and in her maniacally passionate shouts. However, the exclusivity of her being heard belonged only to him.

"Maybe I'm not in love with you, but that does not apply to your... tool" - she whispered to him.

He covered her mouth again and accelerated even more mightily.

Then he stopped for a moment.

Someone knocked again.

One more stroke of inspiration came to his mind of how to shorten the path to her ultimate powerlessness.

He ripped apart one of the hanging towels and made a rope. He tightened her wrists firmly and continued.

He was literally feasting upon her excitement.

"Harder, harder, you fool!" she screamed.

"Let's go to my place" he suggested.

"Wait until I cum - then we'll go."

"You will cum when I say you deserve it. After me."

He untied her. Katya quickly tidied herself up and got ready to leave.

Maxim opened the door.

Three people were waiting in line to use the toilet.

"Guys, didn't you notice the toilet is out of order?" he said in a manner resonating between barely audible and ecstatic..

The bar was as crowded as a beehive.

Jimmy was utterly absorbed by his own guitar.

Robbie, in the role of a bartender busy with work, winked at Maxim, who managed to sneak through the crowd with curved steps and, waving goodbye to the members of the band, made his way through the dark and narrow cobblestone alleys.

***

The sun towered earlier than expected.

The morning seemed to be in a hurry, following the wild rhythm of the city with slightly less grayness than the previous day.

Maxim's modern apartment was located in the heart of

the city and was wide and lavish, appealingly decorated and hastily filled up with expensive sculptures made by blends of marble, copper, bronze and silver.

His irises with the color of the planet, played with the view offered by the highest point of a residential building in the city center.

The road leading to the school across was the traffic circulation - the bloodstream of the city core and there were countless events to be seen every day, which were significant for the shaping of children's characters: from secret signs sent to their crush who remained blind for them, to various ball games, hide and seek, games with marbles; and at night the teenagers were at an all-night guitar playing gatherings, where the first romantic moments occurred.

Maxim lowered the blinds and turned to his muse.

The dream gave out her innocence, her essential, remarkably well-hidden feature.

A lamb in tiger's skin.

He looked at her, his eyes achingly chewing on the knowledge of her transcendence.

His gaze remained focused indefinitely long, maybe hours.

Her existence was the most perfect meditation.

Finally, raising his shoulders, he stretched out and slowly began opening his eyes.

He laid down beside her, helping her awaken.

***

"Stay with me, you, insolent woman" he begged with a melodramatic glow in his gaze.

"You, sir, are crazy" she replied.

"You never explained to me why you don't want us to stay together."

"Huh, are you telling me that you don't see how different we are?"

"In what?"

"In everything. First, you are way too ambitious for me. Second, your eyebrows give away your instability. You are unstable, Maxim."

"My eyebrows?"

"Yes. You know, I can determine the stability of a person by looking at his or her eyebrows. Thick eyebrows suggest stability, while yours... well, the opposite."

"My eyebrows are kinda thin. But..."

"We listen to different music. You do not even know any of my favorite bands. Unlike your friend, you are not part of any subculture, Maxim. You don't have it in you. You belong to crowds of the arts and of the academic circles."

"And?"

"You have no style, man," she said, "look at the way you dress. You're not fucking cool!"

The artist made a grimace looking at his sweater with a picture of Super Mario.

"And you have zero integrity. Every wish that I have you give your best to make come true without objecting. How are you not bored by being so patient, man?"

"I'm this way only with you. But I will change that."

The redhead slowly closed her eyes a little leisurely, with a wandering look, keeping her gaze coldly focused on his eyes.

His pupils have never been wider.

"You know that I would never be able to love you, really. At least not the way you love me. No matter how good looking you are, you don't even attract me physically. You know I'm attracted to ugly and skinny guys."

"I know how disturbed you are, if that's what you meant."

Katya took a pack of cigarettes from her leather bag and lit one up. She sucked heavily on it and breathed out in his face all the smoke.

The artist got very angry and grabbed her by the arm.

"Hey! What the... I'm gonna beat you black and blue! So hard that your mother in law will feel it!"

She looked right through him with a pale and indifferent look.

"I can't understand why all your ex-boyfriends are so... anti-alpha?"

"Anti-alpha?"

"Aha."

"I don't get you."

"When compared, the difference between your self-esteem and the confidence of the ones you've dated differs like in classes. Or at least seems like it, doesn't it?"

The redhead raised her left eyebrow.

"Besides, we talk about fucking introvert dudes with no initiative, charisma, organizational or leadership abilities and a two-way visa to hell and back. These guys got no spirit whatsoever. Just like little boys that have never experienced real crisis."

"If you speak from experience, then you should know that not everyone is like you."

"How the... you're so damn arduous..."

The girl drew the ashtray closer and shook the ashes from the cigarette in it.

"I don't, I don't understand you at all, man."

"What is it that you don't understand?"

"That you are getting from me everything that any man could wish for, and then again you are still dissatisfied. You know we have amazing sex, just what more could you really want?"

"You know the answer very well."

"What?"

"In the material manifestation of this cruel and passing world, only the dedicated warriors of the Impure One appear to be profoundly interested in souls."

"O great warrior of the Impure One who is only interested in my tortured soul, do you really think that your soul could live a life with hallucination?"

"What do you mean? You're not a hallucination, Katya.

Your existence here next to me is real and objective. "

"You know perfectly well of which kind my existence is, Artist!"

"You are no hallucination!"

"And you are mentally healthy!"

An abrupt adrenaline shower poured all across the artist's chest.

"I am your *madness*, Maxim. Your incurable disease."

The redhead extinguished the cigarette.

"You should be afraid of me, you lunatic."

"You are just one immature cock of the walk, Katya. Our biggest difference is that you still live like you're in the high school days. "

"Maybe."

"How could I fall for you so much? Only for you and no one else."

"The devil does not plow nor dig before showing up, O great warrior of his."

"You're telling me this all too late. Besides, it is because of you that I've made a deal with him."

"You did make a deal. But not with him. With Death, dear Artist. You signed up with Death. Remember?"

"What-e-ver."

"What is important is that you did that deal through me."

The artist could see a diabolic restlessness in her eyes. He looked at her for half a minute before feeling the courage to start pulsating through the silence with few deep sighs. All the words of this extraordinarily tired world were superfluous.

He laid down for the second time.

His breathing was deep.. He blinked.

Katya already went away somewhere...

CREATION NO. 1

Following a divine fluency and elegance, the artist's hands shaped the clay mold first, then the ceramic one from which the statue was to be created, using a method known as cire perdue, the lost-wax casting.

It was surreal just like the burning cowls in the chest.

A dedication to Eros.

The labor had no end. The twilights were a new home of madness expressed in the form of an immense passion for the creation-mimesis.

"You are the creation of my mortally wounded and diseased spirit, Katya" he spoke to the hallucination, proudly correcting his half-sitting position.

She usually avoided speaking while the process of creation was taking place.

From time to time she would only throw a sharp look, moving irises coldly, she'd exhale...

He always created his figures while nude. His nakedness was the boat that he would climb into every time he needed certainty along the river-labyrinth that finally would pour into the ocean of his identity.

The one who posed for him, however, hated to be stripped in front of him except during the need of Unity.

He was immensely angry with her.

His feet wouldn't even rise for him to throw an ephemeral

look at the work in creation.

Especially not at the strong, almost rudely prominent vulva, the shape to which he spent indubitably longest time, almost two whole weeks..

He had to imagine familiar shapes of women's curves under the clothes, to add imaginary shapes and figures that pushed and crushed his aesthetic challenges and taboos.

He added wings and a bow with arrow to her like one of the Erotes sculpted in the purest detail to create the most imaginably refined, female version of the Unified Trinity, the multiplied form of Eros for which millennia ago the Gods-maker Hesiod wrote: *Eros* - love, *Himeros* - desire, and *Pothos* - passion, the three merged into One.

He had to stay One even if the One meant renting the mind to the tiny pieces of space not covered by the overwhelming light.

Sometimes he paid more attention to staying One with the darkness without which no existence of light of any kind would've been imaginable.

    ***

One late evening, after many a night like it, the statue divided into parts was ready to be removed from the hardened ceramic mold.

The creation of bronze statues was an exceptional process of many stages of refined creation that the artist experienced as a superb form of self-realization. The extraordinary pleasure with which he conceived his works was the definitive key to success that sustained and fed his reputation as one of the top and most sought-after bronze and marble sculptors, but also generally widely recognized among the top sculptors in the whole country.

Firstly, a thick layer of clay was cast on a combined armature made out of metal and wax, light plastic or hard foam, , which was then to be refined, or arranged in the desired shape.

The precision of the eye, ingenuity, prowess and experience forbid him, like most sculptors, to waste time on developing small-scale models of the statues he imagined, and therefore he immediately began the process of creation into the necessary, usually natural or slightly larger sized composition.

Every detail related to the proportions and placements and as clear as an air in springtime, it shone brightly inside his head.

After many days and, sometimes, many weeks of work on certain details that included constant returning to, redoing and refining, first getting the torso and the extremities, then the head, he would create the desired clay statue, and then leave for the central atelier room where the rest of the equipment for the next continuous stages awaited him.

He would coat the clay statue all over with a thick lubricant enamel to which he would add a three-layer silicone rubber coating which was divided into partitions that were to obtain more parts that could then be welded. After around a quarter of a day, Maximilian would cut off the extra silicone rubber with a thick sharp knife, in half, longitudinally, and then on the segments that marked the places of the desired parts, getting a mold for each one. In one of the three rooms facing east, there was a wood burning furnace, which, besides for heating the room, he also used to melt and warm up the wax, which he then poured into the interior of the silicone molds. Rotating the mold evenly, the wax from each segment was cooled down after twenty minutes and in this way several more hollow wax replicas were obtained.

Then, in the lower part of each segment, he added several wax tubes united in one, the purpose of which was to allow the emission of gases after the spilling of the bronze, but also an even distribution in the mold. Using the tube, the resulting replica was then immersed upside down in the ceramic material, so that the opening was faced upwards.

After this, he brushed the obtained ceramic segments of uneven places and bumps, after which he placed them closely under a jet-stream of a mineral silicate powder which he poured out evenly from the bucket in the middle of the room while there was a protective cover previously placed on the floor.

Next, he would place every segment of the statue inside a special machine that was producing hot steam that melted the wax located in the second room facing east, leaving only a solid, hollow ceramic mold, which he then baked for about two hours at a high temperature, obtaining a solid, definitive ceramic mold.

After finishing with the molding, he could continue the bronze work.

In the third room facing east was the furnace that heated the metals. The bronze was exposed to a temperature higher than the one which the ceramic molds were baked on, after which he would very carefully and slowly pour it into. It only took a few minutes for it to become hardened, after which the ceramic mold could be broken as it was no longer needed.

While returning the various parts of the statue to the atelier, the sculptor did exactly that, using a massive hammer that was blunt on one side and sharp on the other. Holding the pieces with rubber gloves and a protective face mask that safeguarded not only the eyes but the breathing as well, he would turn on the sandblaster- a large red cylinder with a hose, a strong - but not too strong abrasive, crude enough to scratch the bronze, and releasing a sand stream under durable pressure accompanied by low-frequency infrasonic buzzing, he polished it, cleaning it from the mold remnants.

Before going back to the use of the various types of abrasives, he cut and leveled the section where the pipes entered, using a specially designed saw. Then, he leveled out all the little holes, bumps and bulges with a welder to smoothness, followed by another or several rounds of abrasive polishing.

What followed was the welding of all sections together into a single statue. The electric welding machine was composed of a tungsten electrode and a metal cylinder filled with argon and helium, adding in more from the latter whenever a thicker layer was needed.

Finally, before spraying with a substance that was supposed to give the desired color to the statue in the patination procedure, he would briefly spray it all over with fire. Then he would wipe it with a cloth, repeating the same procedure several times.

At the very end, immediately after layering the patina, a thin coat of warmed wax was added with a brush, bestowing the statue almost unearthly, yet natural shine.

The glitter of the freshly cast, polished, patinated, scorching bronze was a dream dreamt by the light in which arms the figure slept awaken.

The artist smiled and, while nodding, made a sign with his finger calling her to come closer - his finger was decorated with a platinum ring with three diagonally placed, parallel rows of bright red tiny rubies. She came.

Fixated into the representation of her re-materialization, her pupils forgot themselves by expanding too far out.

She smiled, and the meaning of that solemn smile was a kiss between the souls.

Eros, incarnated into their joining, was now completed.

He approached the statue that was really a portal.

The next moment entered her, ascending to the promised higher dimension of existence.

He could see her ever-so-clearly! The light represented a golden chain around the soul.

The artist with all the sublime and exalted, natural trembling of the being, began dancing with her.

2. Ludus

INTERMODAL SUNSETS

Maxim's gargantuan atelier took up almost half of a standard sports hall's size, spanning on two floors.

On the upper floor his true home was stationed, a place where he ordinarily slept, ate, performed all physiological needs, organized parties, made love, made plans, as well as sketches for his future sculptures.

The wide hallway divided it into four very spacious and dimensionally leveled rooms and bathrooms together with a toilet.

In addition to the three rooms on the east side of the atelier where he kept the equipment, which was locked with some of his special keys, a significant portion of his time was spent in a room he would normally call a workplace; one that housed hundreds of his drawings, sketches, and mock-ups, at least during the period while he still needed mock-ups.

There was a bed in the study room, too, and the library was also memorable, consisting of over eight and a half thousand books distributed on ninety-eight wooden shelves. Most of the titles were inherited from his father. The number of the ones he actually read was still quite modest.

Unlike his ambitious parent, Maxim never aspired for quantity and whenever he started reading, he was repeatedly plunging into such mental processes that always made him forget about time. The shadow of almost-earthly pleasures, hanging over every page he read, did not allow him to trample on aesthetically perceptible principles. As a self-proclaimed representative of the old reading school, he enjoyed every detail of what he read, and his imagination worked pretty much the same way during his creations.

An unfathomable inspiration for his art was to be found in the wealth buried in its indefinable depth, sometimes an abyss, too. The third room served as a kitchen and a dining room.

The fourth was a guest room and a party venue. There was a large bar in the middle with three modern leather sofas and a party area.

There was also a terrace. There was a huge courtyard around the atelier and a small-sized stable that housed Artemio, a white Andalusian horse. To travel through the woods with Artemio was a thrill experience. In the past, Maxim would rode him for days and sleep in unscathed mountains. After three hours of riding, there was a river and a convenient place to rest.

***

The dawn arrived with a miraculous calling from an underground world that Maxim had just met. The careful watching could reveal scenes of a divine choir hidden in each beam. Maxim woke up fresh with his mind crystal clear, hunting the hidden shapes in the light with a calm smile and a tepid reflection in the soul.

He first noticed the goddess of the earth along with her daughter married to the ugliest of the gods.

Their hair was adorned with vines. As they walked, they made their way through the vineyard they consecrated, followed by three divine figures who drank nectar and ambrosia in peace, weighing the fate of the living beings. Then a few wounded centaurs were coming back either from a battle or from a long journey.

Finally, She appeared, looking so distinct with clearer, brighter face. She was wearing a blue dress. Astonishingly vibrant, and spirited, she was the source of life. Her arms and legs– fascinatingly white and shimmering; each body part wavering, pulsating with tender felicity. Her hair was gold, and the cheeks innocent. She played the harp.

"Katya," he said uncertainly, "is that you?"

"Take me to the Land of Jests," she whispered.

The artist got up and untied the horse. He adjusted the saddle and helped her get up before he sat down himself. The horse went full gallop across the meadow and the road back led through the old pine forest. After a while, he turned to her.

"You look so peculiar. Your arms and legs feel... unreal."

She maintained her indifferent stare at a single point.

"Have you dyed it?" He touched it, "Your hair is golden."

Katya smiled.

"You're beginning to delve into the rest of me, artist."

"This is ..." he said, "your inner child?"

The girl smiled grabbing him wildly by his shirt. Tightening the grip whenever they came across turbulent terrain, he happily hopped into the seat.

Once they found themselves near a clear stream through rocks, with a small wooden bridge, Maximilian began to feel almost pleasant pricking under his right rib and stopped the horse. Katya suddenly jumped off her seat and started running.

"Hey!" clamored Maximilian, getting off himself.

Laughing loudly, she threw a large feather which a moment later was greeted by the tranquil water surface.

"Ah, you..." said Maximilian, "you have no place to run!"

REQUIEM ON A POET'S MAJESTIC END

The poet passed away on the last day of August, a fatefully sizzling day.

He was completely paralyzed, lost his ability to speak.

His own thoughts remained in tune with him and with the inner glory of life after spending the last years in the horrors of a deep poverty.

Maximilian, drowned in the sumptuous fluid tirelessly produced by his lacrimal glands during the moment when, as if they were giving him back to Mother Earth, he thought of the one he met.

It happened in the shittiest hole on earth, a roadhouse.

The drunken Charles, a middle-aged gentleman, didn't have enough cash to pay his bill, so the owner rolled up his sleeves, placing his palm on Charles' cheek in a way only a slap occurs. An awful, feral, unruly slap. The poet grabbed the nearby wooden table and slammed it against the owner's back, remaining with two table legs in his hands. As he made his way to the exit, the furious owner ordered two of the waiters to surround him, and that was the very exact moment when Maximilian recognized him.

While Charles was trying to leave the roadhouse/inn, Maximilian opened the door and pulled him out. Doing so, he locked the door tightly with his both hands holding the latch holding up.

"Fly, oh King of the sky!" he said.

The poet veered his head left and right before taking the fastest step in his whole unwinged existence. A few days later, they met in a narrow road.

"Hey! Paraphrasing savior, come here," Charles noticed him first.

He took him to a nearby cellar and Maximilian tried laudanum and smoked opium for the first time. The poet poured himself an absinthe.

The two sat on velvet two-seaters. The room which atmosphere was defined by the walls decorated with paintings by famous French painters - contemporaries of the Poet – was illuminated by two lamps.

"So, you know who I am," he said at last.

"Yes."

"Then you know that..." he added, "my wings of a giant are bothering me when I try to walk freely."

"Why walk when you are created for heaven?"

The poet smirked.

"Do you believe," he asked, "in ideals?"

"Of course. The belief in better humanity and the harmony between man and nature are paramount."

"Remember, my dear friend, this mankind can not, must not, ever get the best of you. Keep your ideals and loftiness to your own intimacy, serving this humanity the carefully culled garbage that suits it. "

"But Charles... a man will always continue to depend on the civilization. It is a disparate thing when nature oftentimes rewards the wicked, which is why they find themselves in a position to shape our worlds. But I do believe it can be remedied."

"To shape our worlds, you say."

"Yes, Charles, look at your world. By whom is it shaped?"

"You're a fool, too, Maximilian," the Poet said, "first of all, Nature, that monumental sculptor of the body of all beings whose undreamed dreams are called destinies, does not give wrongfully to the wrong. She is no untalented painter to mindlessly disperse Mother Beauty's glittering colors onto the wrong heads. Society is the scavenger that, rinsing up the blood before rising from the abyss of the self-betraying morality with its broken broom, conceded in its blind view, with a painting brush dipping in the swamp of his own primitivism, lies the pigs that they're taking a swim at a picturesque beach. Perversely fluffed standards, not nature, endow the wrong men, my lofty budding young adult."

Maximilian glared at the almostglowing green liquid. Memories, inspired by the words, weaved around every further thought.

"Have you not experienced, if only in a flash, the immeasurable beauty of unquestioned unanimity with Your Work? By God, child, to what you spend your Hope! Do you believe that a more lustful fervor is achievable than Oneness with your truthful, undeniable, self-fulfilled Self?"

"I believe there are certain forces in the Cosmos that, by accident or not, direct our passions to a supreme Good. One that's independent only of our desires and spiritual pursuits. A Good that, one way or another, would ultimately affect us.

A Good that will save us from the tragedy of a deceptive, absurd existence. The name of the salvation on this Earth is Good."

"Every force inside this putrid garbage bin of our Almighty ruler with a surgically removed personality, every force inside this garbage bin you call Cosmos is in an eternal and eternally drunken struggle against each other. But you will start to realize this once you initiate your first Great Work, remember this. And then, only then, will you taste the fruits of your salvation. Just try not to get drunk too early and by someone else."

"You mean, after I create my first Grand Work and witness its reception?"

The poet took a sheet of paper and a pencil and drew an apple.

"What does the apple taste like?"

"I don't know."

"And where did it grow? What is its color? How much does it cost? What, the monkey's fuck, do you know about apples anyway? On what basis are you talking about something you haven't acquainted, young man?"

Maximilian slid into the sheet.

"It was grown nearby the cave outside the city. It has an exceptional green color. One kilo of it costs as much as a glass of green nectar. I know everything and I stand behind anything that's ever become my creation," Maximilian sighed, raising the right corner of his lips.

"For this green nectar or, as I prefer to call it, an elixir of the Word and an artistic wisdom grown on the soil of my Land of Liberty, my dear, no sale price has yet been set, and if it ever happens, I would have to sell your naive hurt soul to this old and cunning demon for whom salvation is not even an abstract noun, and Mephistopheles, Azazel, Baal, Beelzebub, and all the other gloomy majesties of the poetic macrocosm are but disciples which certainly do not share your prowess or your mastery."

The poet poured the green liquid into the young artist's glass. The latter impatiently gulped, shaking his head lively in countless directions.

The poet joined his traditional *pontarlier* glass with his own, put few sugar cubes into two small metal spoons drilled in four places which he placed onto the tops of both cups and lit them. Bringing the cubes together for a moment, the green liquid beneath them also flared up, being a mirror of flame in the poet's eyes.

"You see, dear... this green fairy is not ashamed to ignite her inner fire and prepare our throats for the warmth which they prevent to soberly come out from the depths of our beings by remaining muted filters of her Oneness with the frigidness of your Cosmos whenever she is supposed to be expressed through words. Without her green sorceries they would have remained equally unheard, muting us like the ones for which you are concocting your stupid self-sacrifice and heresy, young man. "

The poet grabbed the two teaspoons, poured the rest of the sugar cubes inside and covered both cups with the apple leaf. The fire went out in a second. At the bottom of both cups there was a thin layer of sugar.

"And now? All that fire, for just a blink of an undrunk eye, loses the battle against a green apple that, for the sake of the truth, is neither poisonous nor causes sin. "

The poet intercepted Maximilian's indefinitely focused eyes for a moment and, closing his own, drank swiftly bottom's up.

"Do you feel ready for self-realization?"

Maximilian, holding his gaze, nodded affirmatively.

"So, your Big Work is on the way. Where is your Muse?"

"She's in my mind."

"With what part of your mind do you conclude that she's somewhere there?"

"She doesn't really exist. Like a verse lost in an unknown abstraction. Like a God undergone lobotomy, sustaining the hopes of the naive."

"The same ones you are striving to save?"

Maximilian crossed his arms wordlessly.

"Maximilian, you remind me of my brother. That stubborn little man with a spirit that's laughing at the face of the physical criteria for spirits. So stubborn that..." the white of his left eye flashed.

"What?"

The poet wiped his eye.

"Are you crying, Charles?" Dazed, Maximilian raised his eyebrows.

"What a flamboyantly pretentious dingbat! He would've

waged a war for a couple of ludicrous ideas to move this society forward... straight into his own chasm... into his damn grave!"

"Is your brother... dead?"

"He is... just... past. And the past is a hazy shadow in an empty skull."

"I'm sorry."

"With that proclivity you have yet to be sorry."

The poet picked up an ivory box from his bag and placed it in the middle of the table.

He opened the box and took out a spirit lamp, a tiny wooden ball with a needle and a polished bamboo pipe with bronze ornaments. At the end of the pipe there was a metal opium-poppy-shaped head, and right in front of the head there were three micro-openings.

The poet lit the lamp, opened the wooden ball and with the tip of the needle took out some of the dark mixture. He held the needle above the burning lamp.

"What happened to him?" Maximilian asked.

The poet held the needle until the slimy, sticky mixture began to bubble in gold paint. He removed the needle and returned the mixture to the ball.

"They killed him."

Mixing the mixture with a needle, he changed the position of the two-seater, leaning on his right elbow. Then he put a bit of the mixture onto the needle again and returned it to the fire.

"Who killed him?"

"The same ones he wanted to enlighten. Dastards to his holy word! The dictators of our standards of living which never threaten their own. And my brother Marcus invested himself, his capacity, and through his own resolution of one of the most serious problems a human being could think of precisely in their study and application.."

The mixture was baked. The poet took it out and made a small ball, which he put inside the pipe's metal head. He returned to the semi-supine state, brought the pipe close to the fire and had a smoke. He kept his eyelids closed for a few moments, then opened them, letting go of the smoke with supernatural serenity and noble zeal in the eyes, in which the pupils strived for complete domination.

"Death," he added.

"Did he solve the problem of death?"

"He was a great scientist, Maximilian. One of the greatest of the century. And believe me, I'm a friend or at least an acquaintance with most of them. "

"So he investigated death. How come?"

"In an extremely non-poetic, and essentially common-sensical way. And that was his heresy. He believed himself capable of describing the most elusive mystery to the finest detail. He created thousands of equations that combined modern knowledge of biology, chemistry, ecology, atmospheric sciences, statistics and combinatorics, botany, bacteriology, entomology, and, hell, whatnot. He also claimed to have the answer to the question of our consciousness after our to-be creators somehow succeeded into conceiving us. He used to say – *we are ever-transforming shapes of the food our mothers ate during pregnancy.*"

"And what is death?"

"He used to compare it with wind, tempest, whirlwind or gail. Whatever is strong enough to tear down the toughest sand towers. The towers where our souls reside or are forced to live. A gail able to turn towers into a sand game."

"Death is a sand game?"

"Death and life both. They have no choice but to play with themselves and with us. We're always in the middle. The idea that we live only once or eternally reincarnate, for Marcus were no more than just an infantile faith that society for which he was a victim is trying to rationalize. To swim across its ocean of ignorance and hypocritical idolatry and reach the promised land of universal wisdom in which the entire Cosmos revolves around all of these wretches. He used to say that the truth is somewhere between the two extremes, with no boundary perfectly defined. Whether, and if so, in what shape we were before coming to life and after it, for Marcus was a play of the probabilities brought by the chaotic wind blowing inward our punctured Cosmos."

Maximilian's face in no way gave away an impression of the sadness the poet inexplicably noticed.

"And as worldly grief pumps the beat of your artistic heart into a perpetual parental pursuit of its children, do you fancy anyone other than Yourself will be able to better understand and play the game of your life and death according to the rules designated by You? Will your Great Work be yours or will it belong to the world you want to save from yourself? In the same arrogant world that does not reckon its own mortality? Carver of alien worlds, do you surmise that this freakish human existence convinced of its immortality would allow a mortal from your breed to save it?"

Maximilian raised a cheek and an opposite eyebrow.

"If you aspire to salvage the world, there is advice for you."

The poet moved the metal part of the pipe closer to the lamp over and over again. The light smoke captivated the views of the artists. Maximilian gasped.

"Be immortal, become a modern God. A Hypergod. Die. Resurrect. Then do a miracle, because resurrection is merely a natural fate. Then do another one. Be sensational in your artistic hypocrisy and salvage this rotten society from itself the way you will salvage yourself."

"It seems as if your brother and me..."

"...are in the same grade of understanding the world until the moment he got poisoned by a rodenticide in them pigshit narcotics. What's missing in your case is to get your works burned before your demise. Certainly, fire shall light your way through the darkness of your superstitions. "

The poet rested his bowed head on the hand that shaped much of the modern times' aesthetic transition.

"Charles... I couldn't imagine you crying."

The poet ironically exhaled.

The artist, impatiently waiting for a subject-changing moment, could no longer restrain himself.

"What was your most substantial inspiration, Charles?"

The poet smiled, turning to one of the pictures. Then poured the green drink in both glasses.

"The aristocrat of letters," he said, "the master of language and style. The one with the memoir beyond his grave. "

"Chateaubriand? You're clowning, right?"

The poet had his indifferent eyes grounded at the pipe.

"I've always regarded you leaning more towards the likes of Poe, Hugo, Champfleury. Your Gautier, get it?! Even Flaubert and Balzac are your more purebred brothers of the pen *than the father of French Romanticism*, your *enemy*, as you called him, re-member?" the sculptor hurried to blurt as much as possible.

"If you had to make a choice between earth, water, air and fire, what would you have been sculpted from?" the poet asked.

"Fire."

"Interestingly, given that mustaches from a vine called drunken thoughts manage to tie your flame up. I am not able to answer anything in addition to what I could possibly hear now. Ask me during my true expressive spawn, and I would surely an-swer differently."

"You find ways to channel your rebellion even through my questions."

The poet uttered an absent monologue: "I'm a gentleman of style, young sir. A responsible stoic, if you fancy. Delicacy is a shadow of my being illuminated by the aristocratic splendor which, as I notice, already caresses your eyes."

"I believe you, Charles."

The glow in the poet's closing eyes rattled through the darkness of the surrounding space like a play of sand corpuscles in the air, going under along every further thought.

THE MYSTERY OF THE TURQUOISE LETTER

That Saturday, the morning crawled shyly from under the cold night cover that the artist had once again trapped inside the cage of his torment, his atelier.

The sun announced the beginning of its all-day-long dominance in the first moments of ray glitter, and then through a triumphant blaze.

Two winterish rays captured the artist's eyes who was sprawled on the pulled sofa.

They came from the window which Venetian blinds looked like upper front teeth from a widely opened mouth..

His smile sprang from the magnificently playful fight with himself.

The dream encompassed an arena in which the only one defeated was time.

His cheeks were grinning.

The eyebrows were dancing in the rhythm of the thoughts colored in his hic et nunc and after few moments, his cheeks scattered up and down to final stiffness with the same wavy tremor. It was his chest's turn. His breath.

The speed range of his breathing was comparable only to that of the light at a time when the eyes in insanity separated him from the road through a distant land which enchantments prepared him for vicissitudes – transitions between love, joy, laughter, despair and fear.

He could hear the beating of a time bomb inside his chest.

"Damn, why don't you leave me alone at least in a dream?" He murmured, rushing to the bathroom, but stumbled upon a nearby chair. The poet's debut book dropped. He got it back to its place and headed to the bathroom.

The ringing of the bell interrupted his intent.

He was completely naked.

He got his pants and a blouse on in a flash and headed back to the front door.

"Good morning, sir. Maxim Comnenius?"A postman stood at the door.

"That's me."

"Great, I have a letter for you," he handed him a hexagonal turquoise envelope made of unique and scented paper interspersed with shades of teal.

Each of the edges was decorated in gold and there were streams of lily blossoms wrapped into a spiral with venomous snakes across the middle.

"Please sign here that you received the letter. Thank you. Have a great day, sir."

The uniformed man hadn't even finished the sentence when his feet proclaimed themselves messengers of his message, leading him down the path that cut the surrounding green areas into perfect halves.

Maxim turned the envelope to the other side. There was a stamp and an inscription:

> *From the One whose nights are but carnivals of your Being.*
> *From the roadside flaneur by fate.*
> *FROM THE HERETIC.*

He curiously analyzed the mysterious thing for only a minute, before running in an unsuccessful attempt to intercept the officer.

There was no one. He sat on one of the wide wooden benches. The lily blossoms looked so mellow.

The artist brought his face closer. The smell was indeed fresh. The colors were vivid. They smelled like a mild dragon blood and cinnabar, two of the ingredients the alchemists claimed that they provide elixir of eternal life through the ages.

"They must've made a mistake," he said as he got up, taking the letter and starting walking.

A construction site was nearby. Around it, a park with a bunch of gallivant kids running in circles and hiding. Their voices were there to vehemently oppose the deafening mechanical noise coming from the construction machinery and the trucks.

Almost unfelt, the smell of the distant sea was dispersed throughout the air.

He passed through the small park and a few lanes below, he reached the post office.

The high metal gate was wide open, and Maxim entered.

No one at the desk. A deafened folk music could be heard coming from an old radio.

"Good day," he said.

No answer.

"Hello, is anyone there?" He asked.

A faint rustle could be heard behind one of the open wooden doors. Shortly afterwards, an old female clerk came out with a strong lipstick and a cigarette in her mouth.

"Can't have a decent coffee pause," she murmured irritated, shaking her cigarette. "How may I serve you?"

"Hi, I need an information about someone who sent a letter to..."

"Boy," interrupted the clerk, "do you really believe we have the capacity or liability to take care of senders?"

"Madam, I just wanted to ask."

The old woman sighed.

"Look at this, the stamp says the letter was sent from here," he handed her the envelope.

The woman pressed the cigarette stub against the metal can and sipped a sip from her coffee before taking the envelope and staring at it for half a minute.

"Lad, please stop joking," she said, leaving the envelope on the desk.

"But ma'am..."

"Please go away before I call security."

Maximilian intercepted her irises with frustration and dismay. Clutching his lips, he turned around/away. There was absolutely no point.

The goggling eyes of the old clerk threateningly measured every movement of the artist who set out to leave half-deliberately, but returned after remembering he had forgotten the envelope. He took it and, with a last glance at the woman who watched in bewilderment, quickly left the room.

THE MARBLE FLÂNEUR

The graves from the Marckest City Cemetery came out shyly from the freezing December fog, peering into the silver sunrise.

It seemed as if the souls of the deceased were spilling over like dimmed birds into the silky vapor dangling over each of the city streets and returned to their eternal resting place after the vapor's dissolution.

Not far from the entrance, in the central right, a monumental black marble structure could be spotted.

The fog left and the graveyard remained snow-covered at ankle height.

A few morning mourners at the tombs were leaving traces, rhythmically tracing the cold air with their breaths.

The cheeks of a middle-aged mother were a hill where the teary streams were slowly drying up, turning into ice crystals.

A few steps from her, stood an older man holding a red bouquet in one hand and a dark blue dress in the other. He spread the dress across the snow-cleansed black tombstone and he put the bouquet in the middle.

Pressing his lips, he turned his head to the entrance where Maximilian was redirecting his own head to the grave he was looking for, and stopped his gaze at the tall black tombstone.

The crunching of the snow sounded almost like the one from the burial.

That tombstone was a human silhouette wrapped around with some object.

Maxim stopped.

In front of him was a statue of a man with his hands in his pockets, and a gigantic open book made of black marble, spread around him like a robe with angel wings.

A message was engraved on the book:

> *Oh flâneur, you who with the acerbity of the Word*
> *trimmed the world garden of unblossoming thorns,*
> *You are missed*
> *by the ones lost in it.*

Searching through the coat, Maxim pulled out a miniature glass bottle and a pack of cigarettes, opened the bottle and a thin stream of greenish liquid poured over the snow beneath the statue. Then he lowered the bottle with the remaining liquid and lit a cigarette.

"Damn you, Charles," he muttered, "the only thing you've accomplished in life are your publications."

The indifferent focus of the eyes intercepted the statues' short, adorned shoes.

He took a smoke and left the cigarette at his foot, slowly peered the decorated stainless-steel rod just above the entrance.

CREATION NO. 2

The frequency of the meetings with Katya had its ups and downs. The second statue progressed slowly and the thorough efforts were limited to his level of experience. The clay model from which the mold was to be made was legless for a long time. The sculptor paid immense attention to each and every anatomical detail, from the glutes to the pint-sized tight joints, to the fingertips.

Katya's second *I* was synonymous with that; and with the innocence engraved in her undisguisedly wet, white eyes.

Maxim finally saw her charming grace in the movements, as if he was endeavoring to emulate it while creating her perfect blend of function and aesthetics. As with all of her movements, there was a perfect cause for the shaping and welding tools, the metal barrel with liquid bronze, the abrasives, the brushes and the pencils he used to mark with.

He greeted the end, spontaneously gawking his mouth open.

The stiff legs caught in the middle of the game illustrated nothing but forceful liveliness.

He had heard an ancient Latin accent a long ago which now resounded in his head: *pulchritudo non est creata, sanabantur.*

Beauty is not created, it is lived.

The beauty of creation was his life.

3. Mania

THURSDAY

The Thursdays were bustling much alike the tongues of the competing grocers, adding simple, easy-to-remember phrases related to prices and the products they sold: Broccoli – your taste buds' monopoly, cucumber – better than a newcomer...

December's air, reflected in a not-so-frigid coolness, blended into the atmosphere of the remote suburban villages.

Behind the market there was a small and compact cafe with a rectangular Dutch garden with densely planted, colorful tulips, anemones, and snowdrops.

Here Maxim, sometimes, alone, while listening to evergreens of his youth, would've allowed the vortex of unending thoughts to fly out of his mind's nest at the day's beginning.

The day was unusually warm and bitter, like coffee. The sky – completely empty.

This time Jimmy was sitting next to him, having his usual caffè corretto with cognac. They were playing chess.

Jimmy got the metal figures and the board from Mariana for his birthday.

"The new album's gonna be the bomb," he said, moving the black bishop on C5, "you must come".

Maximilian almost sourly raised his lip and his left cheek, exhaling inertly. The D5 pawn was blocking several attack strategies. He decided to make a sacrifice.

"Thank you for the invitation".

"It's not an invitation. I said you must," Jimmy said half-ironically, making up for the lost pawn.

"Alright then."

Jimmy recalled some of the melodies that could be heard in the background. The hands on the chessboard played on their own.

In one of the corners, middle-aged man and woman were drinking their morning coffee. The man was wearing gold-plated glasses.

"I'm telling you, I can't consider that approach ethical, after all" he added.

"We're talking about a starting point treatment, in addition to the regular antipsychotic therapy. If additional necessities are pointed out, as you know, it will undergo adjustments."

The woman thought for a moment.

"And did I tell you he first appeared to her on the same date when her husband died?" she asked, lighting a cigarette.

"Her real husband?"

"Yes. Two years later."

"What are you talking about?!"

"It's as if the trauma has opened a portal to some supernatural or telepathic force."

"Or maybe a subconscious one... and how did he appear?"

"She said he was a little shy and smelled of incense. He fled and hid from some freaking aliens with roasted feet which then kidnapped him."

The man startled, almost dropping the coffee.

"Roasted?"

"Yeah, their feet looked and smelled like fried burgers."

"Oh God," said the man, frowning, "was she hungry?"

The two light-heartedly giggled, and then returned to the seriousness of their conversation.

"Jokes aside, we are talking complex schizophrenic hallucinations, and this is surely the first time I, personally, have come across something like this."

"Me too," the woman said, "as you know, trauma plays a crucial role in activating motivation and triggering connections, so I always try with my patients, with the help of psychodynamic therapy, to dig deeper into their memories. Sometimes, in a combination with therapies that involve expressive art, keeping diary of thoughts, emotions, and dreams, and aided by psychosocial strategies, I try to point out that even above these complex hallucinations, a control trigger can be established with the help of a disciplined day-to-day solutions to the repressed motives behind them. And with exceptionally strong and sustainable self-discipline, even hallucinations such as these can only be interpreted as an isolated, sometimes completely transient, stage."

"I agree," the man added, taking off his glasses, "thus encouraging dealing with the internal and deep causes, while giving the subject disciplining and socializing tasks through external activities."

"Exactly".

The cautiously eavesdropping Maximilian scratched his left forearm, drinking his last sip of coffee, making the final move with the queen.

"Checkmate".

Jimmy was slowly finishing his cup of corretto and, as if surprised, furrowing his eyebrows, and raised his cheeks.

"You are aware that chess is in my heart," Maximilian winked.

"You sound like a whining teenage girl after losing her virginity," Jimmy sighed in disappointment. "You're just a disciplined soldier who sees and does things to the end."

"I can imagine how hard it is to always lose. Can't know exactly, but I can imagine."

Jimmy laughed ironically.

"Let's go," he removed all the heavy metal figures from the table and began placing them inside the chessboard.

"All right, just a sec," Maximilian rummaged in his wallet.

"Just enjoy your victory while it lasts," Jimmy interrupted him.

Maximilian's ears were still tuned into the intriguing conversation from the table across.

"We both agree that a person's self-destruction is a sad, tragic outcome," said the woman. "Her super-ego from the very beginning was largely materialized in the image of her dead husband, while the Id in the hallucination of extraterrestrials."

"Interesting idea, Andrea. However, chances are we would not have been able to resolve the issue even if we acted immediately."

All the figures were inside.

Jimmy took the board, left money on the table, and then they both left.

THE FLIGHT OF
THE ALBATROSS

It was late. Maximilian had to get ready for tomorrow's serious amount of work on the new sculpture which he did not wish to separate even physically.

And yet, the boiling of all that energy actively kept him alert and far from exhaustion.

Katya, unlike Maximilian, appeared really tired; her hair in many shades, from flaxen to dark amber, was unkempt.

"Please leave me, I need rest."

"Guess who needs it more," Maxim said, "you are inside my mind, I am not inside yours."

The girl glanced at him.

"OK," he said leaning over to the other side of the sofa, and grabbing the poetry book which the Poet made his debut many years ago.

"The Poet died at forty-six. I have twenty-six. We were born on the same date. His sunset is the horizon where I dig up my sunrise's gold", he said to himself almost chuckling.

His eyes shone like the windows that broke the sunrays of every sunrise precisely over them and exactly when his dream was most needed.

The turquoise hexagon-shaped envelope was placed on the nearby desk.

Humming unfamiliar rhythmic melodies, Maximilian got up from the couch and climbed up the stairs to get whiskey. He came carrying a large bottle of four-year-old Kentucky bourbon and poured himself a glass.

Looking keenly at the envelope, he spilled a few drops on the floor, muttering to himself incomprehensible phrases that resembled a prayer. Then he swallowed quickly.

There was something in the damn envelope.

He got closer to it.

He made a sluggish semicircle with his irises from one to six o'clock. Reaching out with his hand, he tried to pick the envelope up; there was something underneath. When he rubbed it between his thumb and forefinger, the envelope split in two. Under the turquoise one, there was another, identically-sized, hexagonal ocher envelope.

"What?" He muttered. "Another one?"

He took both envelopes, holding them tightly.

He slowly brought them closer to his eyes and started opening them.

Both opened from the inside. The odd opening mechanism implied one of the edges should be pulled out from under the center to open the inside.

The sound of the paper was a mixture of painful screaming and comforting, almost soothing white noise.

The turquoise envelope was finally open.

He grabbed the other one and quickly pulled it away, leaving that one open, too.

The latter smelled of rain, not just any rain, but the one that oftentimes fell in the city park amidst the zenith of the children's games.

"Hey, are you going to pour me some of that scotch?" Katya woke up.

"That's bourbon. You're not into sleep tonight, are you?"

Maxim left the envelopes on the sofa, took a glass and supplied the whiskey.

Maximilian's gaze commented on Katya's drinking agility, which equaled each of her movements.

"That's bourbon, Kat-ya. Chill."

"I'm not your Kat-ya, you son of a..." she replied sleepily, "what kind of bourbon is this?"

"I believe a Buffalo Trace, I believe it blends some barberry, barley and cashews flavors."

"I get its taste," Katya raised her right eyebrow, "the barley's somehow hardy. Not that bad, though. It was about time for you to hit the target. But it's still better with caramel."

Maximilian left the book aside. He pointed his head at the space that covered the two sculptures.

"And them?"

"What about them?"

"Don't you think I've hit the target with them?"

"Hmm, it's not bad for now."

"If it was bad, I wouldn't have experienced you so clearly, unlike the first time."

Katya curved the ends of her lips half-ironically.

"You know what I start thinking when I'm fed up with everything? That even someone like you could be freaking capable of fulfilling an agreement," he said.

"Hmmm..." mumbled the girl thoughtfully, "as an intellectual it would be more practical at times to think of the pain of crashing to the ground."

"What?"

"The dragon kite is no longer able to fly once it escapes the thread."

"I'm not a dragon kite."

"But a logorrheic parrot locked in a cage?"

The artist's gaze fixated on one of the sculptures.

"I'd say albatross."

"Be careful not to get yourself on a deck so the crewmen break your giant wings, o vast sea-bird."

"If I was you, I'd be careful about the way I'm getting in and out of my life," Maximilian said, "I am capable of flying through it, but for you... for you it's just a giant maze. One that could gobble even you."

"Sounds like fun!" Katya grinned. "Overestimation is a bad, bad thing, bird! Artist!" She added. "Able to carelessly hit back. To make twaddle like a sailor on a stray ship."

"You don't say?" Maximilian turned around, waiting for her affirmative nod.

"You are now babbling about your own world, and then about the world around you. And you should always watch out for the latter."

Maximilian smiled sourly as he approached her.

"Am I twaddling again, or does this indeed sound a bit like... a threat?"

The girl, watching in a focused manner, distorted her glaringly crimson lips in the right corner, nodded and suddenly disappeared in the darker parts of the room.

The sculptor was left alone.

He languidly picked up the two envelopes and took out the letters. The handwriting seemed familiar. Murmuring through his nose, he looked through them, hastily eye-chasing the words and throwing the letters on the sofa.

"Hmmm... a divine heretic," whispered to himself, pouring whiskey, "as if I didn't have enough divine ups and downs, U-turns and less divine, and in fact, diabolically much work to do."

He turned his head towards the space between the two sculptures.

There was a humble pedestal of black marble on which was laid an indefinable and newly started oval object.

***

The challenge of working late at night was a tempting endeavor where the artist left his thoughts at times to sail, at times to burn and ignite, at times to balance their inaccessible essence, shaping the whole exterior by their own example.

Certainly, he was nowhere close to an emblematic night bird, but the moments when his thought-voyage was truly emanating were mostly nocturnal; maybe that could've explained why the mornings were becoming shorter and shorter, adjusting the biorhythm to their motives for aesthetic self-realization.

The day passed peacefully.

The city's arteries seemed clogged by the fog of the factory chimneys in the outskirts.

Maximilian slept on the floor. His tools, pieces of black and white marble, and metal rods were scattered all around and the very offbeat placement of his body gave the impression that he had fallen asleep working.

Under his eyelids, his irises circled like tiny, round furies.

The heartbeat fleeted; even his right hand, clenched into a fist, began to tighten and release alternately.

A thin stream of water flowed from the inside of his eyes as he occasionally pressed his eyelids. He accelerated his breathing, gradually orienting himself towards both inhalation and exhalation from the mouth.

"Madman... I don't think so!" He said in a dream, continuing his cacophony of unarticulated sounds until the words "heretic" and "dead" were uttered clearly, and then a sudden scream followed. A moment later, rolling his eyes, he straightened up in a sitting position.

"Fucking hell".

In these recent times, nightmares begun haunting him like a bunch of wild dogs – a consideration that produced stimulus for developing a habit of keeping a dream diary.

"What a suave con artist" He chuckled to himself staring for a moment at the envelope from which two white hexagonal papers peeked through.

He got the glue out from the left drawer of the shabby tools-only cupboard, and carefully glued the two envelopes.

His very gaze seemed blurred by the ambiguity of the obsessive ideas.

Slowly, he came near the wooden window and opened it. The day was just passing. He went back to the dried envelopes and, carrying them to the window, began to tear them.

The bitsy pieces of paper swayed in the wind, dissolving their scents with those that sailed from all over the city, and Maximilian believed could be distinguished in detail thoroughly only by using his sharp nose.

Pulling on a shirt and trousers, he hurried to make coffee, which he planned to drink in a walking-mode.

He opened the notebook in which he wrote down the memorized bits of his dreams and quickly added a few short sentences.

On the way out, he looked with a dim gaze to the wide mirror with a wooden frame which he once made.

Applying a thin layer of hair gel, he combed and parted his dense dark hair to the right. He put on a winter coat, a woolen scarf, his favorite crocodile leather green-brown shoes, before tranquilly leaving the studio.

While walking, his gaze was once again fixed, only this time on an indefinite point halfway to the lowest point to which his motionless eyes had reached. Not blinking for several minutes, he moved his lips smoothly, sometimes joining them together at the top, as if trying to talk.

Suddenly, a large, brown, shaggy chocolate retriever came out of nowhere and started barking as if the devil himself was to be chased. The feeling of stun ended in a moment of an ill-fated try to hit it with his shoe until the shoe fell away in the very attempt to untie it, with him almost falling in a super-silly and amusing way.

"Damn you! Both you and that crazy heretic! Dumb mules!" He shouted removing the scarf from his mouth, swaying for the second time towards the terrifically agile dog, which, spreading its scattered bark, was already leaving. It reminded him of an old city rascal that once, many years ago, attacked him as he rode back to Jimmy. A close encounter left a scar in the shape of a human ear or half of a heart on his leg.

For a moment his face turned red, and his breathing resembled one that'd be typical in a nightmare. The street was almost entirely devoid of people, and the faces and looks of the few passers-by were devoid of expression.

After around sixty steps, there was a house enclosed with a high hedge from where a middle-aged woman hastily approached. Looking away for a moment, Maxim met her eyes. The same woman from the bar the other day. The doctor.

Maximilian diverted his gaze to the wide, white-painted tin where an inscription could be seen:

Psychological Counseling Center **Urania**
Holistic Psychotherapy Management
Dr. Andrea Morris

The barely visible telephone number was under the inscription.

The artist focused his gaze on the three children playing ball in the middle of the empty street.

SWERVING OF A STUNTED ART

For the next few weeks, with a deeply profound sense of primordial curiosity, the earthly urges revived some of the forces that prompted his life-giving spirit.

It was late Saturday night in early January when Jimmy and his band *Sagittarius* finished their concert.

The guests dispersed and the large smoky hall in the cabaret club, with dominating red walls and curtains, remained almost empty.

Simon, the green-haired bassist, turned off the main lights.

The male members of the band – Jimmy, Sylvester the drummer, Philip the keyboardist, and Simon, got entirely surrounded by girls with lipstick, short skirts and some of them, with accentuated stockings Alexandra, Maxim's colleague from the Academy's postgraduate studies; Emma, her close friend; Ivana; Helena; Anna and Christina; promoters and friends of the band's members.

Mariana, the blonde composer and the blue-eyed singer, shared the booth with Maxim.

The whole music of the Sagittarius Band was her creation.

There was a paper towel on the table where Maxim

poured white powder which Mariana turned into five lines, holding a thin paper tube in her right hand and a ruler in the left.

"A five-line staff," he said with a half-smile, "wanna go first?"

Maxim nodded as he approached one of the lines. Mariana handed him the paper straw and he sniffed strongly and fast.

He returned the straw to her and she held up her head over the powder.

"How are you guys?" Jimmy's voice could be heard from the other side of the compartment. "Shit's strong, isn't it?"

"You could've found something cleaner!" Mariana shouted angrily.

"Cleaner, my ass. Look how clean you are, you rascals! You, Mariana, still smell of sweat, and who knows whose."

"And you stink of your sense of humor."

Jimmy smirked.

"Snobbish weirdo," she murmured before taking a line, wrinkling her entire left half of her forehead.

Maxim still felt the overwhelming breach of MDMA through his nostrils, visualizing his own aura of colors that defined euphoria, changing from moment to moment as he merged with the substance.

"I wish I wasn't so desperately alone," Mariana said with a sigh.

The male members of the band and the girls left the spacious room, taking their places in the neighboring booths surrounded by long red curtains.

Jimmy got out hugged by two brunette girls. The three were laughing out loud on some politically inspired jokes until one of the girls closed the blind.

The others continued the hilariously loud conversation.

The almost comatose green-haired bassist Simon, with his head tilted and his nose pierced, moved too phlegmatically and loosely to talk.

Sylvester was about to whisper a secret message to a girl, when he delivered a sensual bite on her ear, gently holding her neck.

Philip, with a somewhat inspired gaze in his eyes, at first uncertain, put his fingers inside of one of the girls' panties. The other girl didn't seem interested.

Mariana saw her reflection inside Maxim's bright eyes. She looked playful. Some of her own movements seemed larger than she imagined.

The advancing of the effect seemed to mean an ever-stronger glow in his large eyes.

"Why are you..." he leaned toward her, "alone?"

The girl's gaze was almost confused, exclaiming in flabbergast.

"What do your folks do?" he added a second question, just an instant later.

She smiled cutely, succinctly staring at him before getting her natural gaze.

"My folks?"

"Your ma and pa, of course."

"Got no idea know what it is they could be doing. I'm not on good terms with my father."

"Why?"

"I used the lemon squeezer repeatedly after use, without washing it."

Maximilian burst out in laughter.

"What's so funny?" She asked angrily.

"Are you telling me that you're serious about not having a good relationship with your father because of such nonsense?"

"Yes, absolutely! And after retiring, he withdrew from any social engagement and became a courtyard bird with stunted wings that cannot see a thing beyond its own beak. It's just awful how alienated he became from the whole world."

"Okay," the artist muttered.

"Oh, and he didn't let me enroll in art school. He regards life as a fucking chess match."

"Is he a chess player?"

"Grandmaster. Active. Did I mention he's Russian?"

"Damn, so that's why you're a composer. I see the similarity between chess and making music."

"I wanted to paint and act and..." she pursed her lips, "and sometimes I did it during lectures."

"And your mother? What's your relationship like?"

"I see her twice a year. With no specific opinion about her, I don't really know how she's doing."

"Twice a year?"

"They're divorced," Mariana whispered, bringing her knees closer, "and I live with Dad."

"Sorry."

"I am sorry you're so damn naive, Maxim. And now I gotta move."

"What? Are you going?"

"Yeah."

Maximilian moved his body towards hers and pulled her down, towards the leather chairs, forcing her to sit down.

"Wait a minute, stop," he put his hand around her shoulders, "what's wrong with this conversation?"

"Nothing."

"Well? Are you gonna leave me these lines?"

"Can't do 'em anymore," she said, "and everything's linear for you anyway."

"But I've seen you..."

"Ecstasy makes me want to have sex. And I have no one to do it with and I don't really feel like suffering."

"You really do suffer," Maximilian said smiling, blinking almost into her eyes.

The girl smiled wistfully.

"And you really do want to help me overcome life's suffering."

"Wide-heartedly."

"Wide?! ..." the girl burst into deafening laughter. "You're insane, dude!"

Maximilian also laughed, spontaneously starting to hug her.

"Chances are, you will find yourself... one day."

"If someone needs to donate you a heart, just say so with no feeling of shame. Deal?"

After a few minutes, they both lost themselves in laughter.

The night was long and spirited.

***

Maximilian's energy level was slowly waning along with the night. The substance that at first propelled his blood vessels, after a few hours left him at the mercy of the remaining awareness.

The variety of thoughts, memories, and visions that flowed through his mind was slowly expanding and growing, weakening his control over his own will.

Leaving the bar, he headed in an unknown direction.

His eyes clung clumsily as he stumbled or kicked with his shoes in the obstacles on the winding, narrow sidewalk, so he walked more slowly, ungainly arching his arms in order to support himself in case he hit somewhere.

His whole walk was like stepping on a thin wire stretched between reality and dream.

Before getting overwhelmed once again by spontaneous flashback-like flow of memories of different life periods, he thought about whether it was possible to actually be awake or not.

"Watch out, albatross, and be careful not to get drunk from your vanity and fall on a deck, so that sailors-gloaters would break your wings," Katya's voice echoed.

Keeping his arms straight, he wouldn't let himself fall. Even if he did, his wings could not get broken. His wings painted the art that gave birth to the one who dared command and, unfoundedly, unwarrantably criticize because of her own surges of inner resentment and insecurity. The albatross was Her. Or not? After all, the albatross was a graceful flyer and the king of the great wide open. A Conqueror of sublimity.

She never reached for the heights of this world and beyond with all its width; she was closer to a regular, everyday mockingbird. One that hid her cowardice and fear of facing the world, and ever-more unskillfully, with the thick fogs of her desperate lifelong cynicism.

That is why she does not even exist in this world.

Fear doesn't allow her physical existence in a world that's not sculpted for her. So, when she realized her inability to cope with the coldness of a distanced world, she decided to settle down in someone else's head.

Ah, if she just for a moment, falls into his hands!

A peacock was following Maximilian since the end of the park. Where did it think he was going? Probably it thought the artist would not notice its concealed presence. It was lying itself, of course.

Maximilian first walked as if in delirium, but his step gradually stabilized. Turning back from time to time, he quietly whispered incomprehensible words, uncrackable passwords.

For a short time, unbreakable peace reigned in his mind and body, the moment he saw the miraculous bird in million vivid colors as he was leaving the neighborhood where the Poet had his final somersault towards wreck and the world of stray souls that he so unyieldingly struggled to disguise with doses of elegance, flaneurism and bohemianism. He did not belong to that wicked hole. He represented a world in which bright people like him were quickly extinguished along with the last sparks of hope for the salvation of all that made the world lifeworthy. A world in which only courtesans, robbers, drunkards and gamblers lived their cause known only to themselves. The peacock appeared from the alley of the courtesans.

The moment it was noticed it seemed dark, reminiscing those dark-skinned courtesans with whom the Poet sometimes spent his already useless, precious piece of life. Or those two prostitutes from the club that hung out with Jim, who was a wandering seeker on the other side of the border beyond the limits of mischievous amusement and impairment.

Spinning his head towards a newly appeared shadow in front of the spy bird, Maxim failed to hold himself still as he hit, a metal pedestal with his fingertips where a drunkard left an empty cognac bottle. The artist fell, the breaking of the bottle to pieces could be heard in a buzzy auditory disarray.

His pants got slightly torn at his left knee and his palms were slightly scratched, while, using his unmistakable reflex, he cushioned the fall.

"Boneheads! You'll regret everything!" he shouted loudly as he rose to his feet. He grabbed the broken bottle by the neck with his hands and put it in his pocket. He tidied his clothes with his scratched palms and continued while breathing angrily and swiftly. His nostrils were widening, as were his pupils. All of his hair seemed to get bristling. His face was flaring. The bird was not there. He could feel every current and vibration in the air, every whisper. The senses were as if borrowed by another-world's traveler. Slowly, without twisting his body or his eyes, he trod in the cursed bird's direction. He walked slightly, turning to the course of the shadowy cobbled street until he finally reached the two maple trees on the crossroad.

Some ghostly and inhuman sounds were coming from a bush. Holding his head slightly to the right, he walked warily. A hilarious alloy of animal laughter and screams deafened Maximilian's hearing.

The mysterious bird, a fascinating artifact of the near-absurd festivity game in which nature juggled with melanin, now, for reasons as inexplicable as a moment earlier, hid behind a dense bush that seemed to have spread its feather-leaves. Maximilian paused for a moment to take a far-reaching look under the luminescence of a distant streetlight that was almost stunned by the endless twirling of innumerable flying insects. He noticed a brightly glittering beak. He advanced to the bird, taking the hand out of his pocket with the brightly shining object.

NOTES FROM THE EDEN OF FLAWLESS REVERIES: CREATION NO. 3

The world of Maximilian Comnenius was an unconquerable ocean, where the hard-waving ships that carried a peculiar imagination were sinking deeper and deeper, floating in their own whirlpool.

His heart was pounding with the power of the warm and world-conceiving Sun; since the very first few seconds of the sunrise, he could feel the gentle warmth that radiated from the inception of a new day inside his head.

He opened his eyes slowly, blinking confusedly.

Inside the atelier, he was completely naked, like when he was creating his sculptures. Exhausted. With enough self-control so as not to feel utterly scared, although shivering to the last cell.

He could not recall how or when he arrived.

Gaping with his eyes, he scratched the back of his head and put on a T-shirt, and underpants from the nearby closet.

There was no choice; he had to put on some old, stained

"

pants and knotless speckled shirt, gifts from an ex-girlfriend.

He looked in the mirror - he was as colorful as a peacock.

A peacock! The stalker bird touched by the very last memories.

For a moment, he turned his gaze to the seemingly strangely enlarged third sculpture, and in the next minute, he redirected it back to the window. Inside shone the glossy, thick leather cover of his dream diary behind the glass.

He almost forgot to write down his last dream.

Opening the showcase's window, he took the notebook with an ink pen attached to it, and started writing:

"January 3rd and still not a sign of snow. Yesterday the sky and the clouds were white. They said it would snow a bit, but I know it is still early.

Late in the evening I was followed by a peculiar colorful bird, a peacock. Due to my slightly excessive intake of ecstasy, I do not remember it quite clearly.

But that is why I remember the dream.

At the café, Dr. Andrea said that it is helpful to write down dreams, therefore I will do so.

The odd fellow from the last few dreams reappeared, whom I did not mention in this diary until now, only out of fear for my own life and my own mind.

I am afraid he would punish me in one of the following dreams as I am writing this.

Or confront me with something I do not even know that exists.

The sinister figure introduced himself as The Heretic, firstly appearing through letters.

He then added that he is capable of contacting me in any way he chooses, and this time he decided to do so in my sleep.

In a quite uncanny way, he claims to be a divine and celestial being with the aptitude to enter my mind unhindered, to read and sometimes control my thoughts.

He calls me Enoch, after a biblical saint.

Deep down, I am at least partially heartened by the hope of being wrong about all this, as well as his existence, which is one of the reasons that prevents me from putting an end to my earthly torment and passing on to a world that, in his words, is nonpareil.

After all, he has invited me several times to join him.

In such a world of unrivaled beauty, he claims, alcohol, nicotine, drugs, immorality and abomination are forbidden.

That is why in yesterday's dream he forbade me to do things that would lead me to immorality, which, in turn, would prevent me from entering this Caelum.

I hope, indeed, that The Heretic will have an understanding for this diary note."

Maxim closed the journal and returned it safely to the showcase. He was terribly thirsty and, humming a monotonous melody, ran to quench his thirst.

At the same time, he put water in a pot to make coffee and put it on the old, and, at places cracked and rusty, stove.

He walked back, drinking his coffee.

The water was splashing on the stomach walls with each and every new step.

Sitting down, he took the smartphone, opened the phone book app and started scrolling. He stopped at the sixth name: Andrea.

Insecure, he raised his head and left the phone on the table. He stared blankly at the ceiling, feeling the flow of his own blood through the back of his neck, culminating in a warm sensation around the top of his head.

After a little while, he lowered his head. The new sculpture gave a somewhat different impression this time, so he got up and stood right in front of it. Breathlessly, he analyzed every bit with full concentration.

Carefully, and as slowly as he could, he raised his eyes: the feet, the calves, the knees, the thighs, the stunning buttocks, the hips, the pelvis and the exposed intimate parts, the waist, the stomach, the back, the ribs, the chest, the arms... her arms There was something peculiar, an abstract and inexpressible mystery in those seemingly gentle hands like wings that epitomized all the panache of the movement they were hinting at.

Her hands were pointed at an unknown forbidden fruit.

The statue seemed like it was reaching for something, not less habitual or usual than itself, perhaps for wisdom and sagacity from a faraway world or some extraterrestrial panacea, an empyrean wizardry.

Maxim sat on the floor, relying with his whole weight on the creaky wooden chair.

He memorized impeccably all the moments spent on bringing the work into existence, all except for one.

He could not, even from the nethermost layers of his being, find the strength to extract the moments from his memory while shaping its hands.

The only thing he could remember was that he had deliberately left her handless so that he could further focus on shaping the most satisfactory hands imaginable, based on the very same principle he exploited in the previous two sculptures when he created the absolute intimacy and sublime legs.

With each subsequent sculpture, he hoped to perfect the creation of one specific body segment. He turned his eyes to the other two sculptures, contemplating and observing all three creations.

The water was boiling. He ran to the stove and took his coffee a moment before it spilled, poured it into a cup and returned, leaving it on the chair.

The natural scent of the medium-light Brazilian Santos coffee permeated lavishly every segment of the air with supernatural, dazzling freshness, surpassing the combination of fragrances of marble, glue and metal.

Maximilian went on analyzing his latest venture.

The inner whisper of the question echoed loudly to him: *how is it possible I have created the most graceful arms and hands I have ever seen?*

He couldn't believe the sight that captured the imposing bewitchment of a work of art that had never come to his cognizance before.

"Hell, can't remember how, but... I contrived to convey all the ravishing details of the idea. Katya, you are a petrified form of my unspoken feelings and unfulfilled lusts."

Suddenly he felt a touch on his shoulder.

"Are you proud, you fool?" she asked, raising her cheek. His gaze was fixed.

"Watch out, one of the stray angels also bragged forgetting himself up in the sky, and eventually stumbled and fell. He now lives in eternal solitude and in the murk of his own illusion of righteousness, pulchritude and truth."

"I'm not an angel."

"It seems your creative genius would like you to be."

Katya stepped forward, stopping right next to the central statue. Maximilian got up and took the cup of hot, fragrant coffee, at the same time remembering to reach for the phone he had put in his pocket.

"Hmm, this sculpture is somehow... too similar to the previous ones."

"Yes?"

"Yeah."

The sculptor looked up.

"I don't see the problem with the similarity, as you call it, if the quality is..."

"The quality is the same, young gentleman," she interrupted, "and I thought we agreed to work on a constant meliorism, an ongoing upgrade celebrating the nascence of each new work instead of upgrading the ego."

„Pulchritudo non est creata, sanabantur. Beauty is not created, it is lived. "

"You are too much in love with the concept of living your own reflection, artist. And art is neither a reflection nor the water in which you see it, and which can so easily drown you."

The sculptor blew carefully into the coffee, ruminating about the bubbles from the ends, forming imaginary universes.

"And now?" He asked.

"Now," Katya said, "the fog of your sketchy imagination will envelop all of what I live, until your abilities to reflect Love in the outside world reach the Eden of its insights again. And until then, Narcissus, try to indulge into your own reflection... differently."

"Hey, seriously?! You are leaving me?"

"No, halfwit. Don't you remember the agreement?"

"I don't know if I remember."

"You're lying," Katya said quietly, gradually changing her shape.

"What?" Maximilian asked, putting the coffee away.

In a few moments, Katya's face began to fade and fade, as if evaporating.

"What the...?" Maximilian asked in disbelief half-limply, following his own shock of frantic screams of helplessness that drowned his reach towards the miraculous figure whose shape was finally stabilizing.

"You're not the same?!" he approached her from behind.

The foggy figure, resembling a statue, stood perfectly in its center, motionlessly illuminating the atelier, radiating an elusive white light reflected as a translucent spirit or a transcendental cosmic angel in the artist's emerald irises.

4. Storge

EMPYREAN

The day seemed pretty calm once again. Once again, he could not recall the dream. A few moments after waking up, the echo of the blurred dream phantasms haunted him until he pulled the massive Venetian oak blinds that so often and so vividly brought him back to his childhood past in church.

They resembled incredibly those in the room where he was once locked up after one of his little mischiefs. Offended by one of the girls to whom he presented his best drawings, he cursed and was heard by Eurosina, the youngest nun, who said she would cut out his tongue if he ever dared to utter such words again in her presence.

Right after lifting the heavy blinds, Maximilian embodied the whiteness of the outside world that the snow so selflessly and gallantly served to the world in the palm of its hand.

Maximilian opened the diary where, in addition to his dreams, he occasionally wrote down his experiences, perceptions and plans, and began to write:

"In the last few days, the heretic seems to have withdrawn. I am hopeful that Dr. Andrea's words from the café are in place and his existence in the dream world is limited and all this is just a phase.

I now feel more alive, unfolding in the middle of this

winter's first snow.

Tonight, Jimmy and his band are about to have their first album promotion.

Tonight, I will spit in the face of the heretical demon that haunts me before I hear the dull bang of his ugly head on the disco podium where I'll make my performing debut as a backing vocalist.

I'm looking forward to the next entry in this diary! "

***

The club was spacious enough to accommodate over three hundred adolescents and slightly older bachelors who enjoyed the show of the guys on stage.

Jimmy tested the endurance of the new guitar with his thunderous madness on the strings.

Mariana was playing and dancing all over the stage with rhythms that dictated the audience core liveliness. Without a microscopic grain of white dust that traced the way to energy and euphoria for the other members of the band, she imposed radiant energy in the performance.

Ian, the bassist, handed out a dose to everyone just before the concert, following the unwritten rule in cases of tours and dynamic periods when the band was preparing for more performances.

Until the very end, the whole band was carried away by their own allurement of the impeccable performance, gratefully perceived and reflected on the no less spirited audience.

Maximilian, while making his stage debut, experienced for the very first time an exchange of vigor and energy with such a mass of jumping and deranged teenagers. Until that moment, he could never have imagined the sundry facets of the process, the dichotomy of which, until then, he had only assumed.

Gradually sinking into the atmosphere, his thoughts played to the rhythm they reflected, once again, dictated by him.

Unstoppably harnessed in the relaxed omnipotence that emanated from the substance, the currents seemed to still leave marks on his veins, and he went wild more than everyone else.

The possibility of the change he lacked in his life was no longer just an unmarked path through the perpetually foggy infinity, but a feeling. A reality that those few moments could be experienced with their hands outstretched to the limitless void that no one else in the room could see, less touch.

For a moment, Maximilian felt light as an angel who skillfully and persistently penetrates the clouds, knowing how to apportion them and make a complex network of roads between them. At times he did not waste a single moment on the crossroads; he immediately chose the direction.

Each choice reflected the sheer, absolute truth. Truth, an actuality to stay alive for, just like the way the audience was alive.

The scent of the varnish that coated the tall scarlet mural that morning drilled powerfully through Maximilian's nostrils.

And at the moment of hinting that the countless stimuli will perfectly coalesce into an experiential Oneness and a feeling of omnipotence of presence, concentrating the gaze on an undetermined point towards the exit, some mixed cries began to echo.

Mariana's eyes stopped, too.

The other members of the band raised the tempo.

The windows in the adjoining spaces vibrated slightly from the peak of the transient rock polyrhythm in which, in addition to the tempo, like the composer herself, the volume was constantly fluctuating.

Maximilian was hovering all over through his smile like an angel. In a split of a second he realized his unfulfilled piety and a complete empyrean serenity. The Empyrean followed him wherever he could bring it. For the sake of the purity of the moment it was irrelevant to ask questions that touched the audience's sudden panic and escape to the exit, or why Jimmy threw the bag with the magic powder in the ventilation hole in the middle of the concert, or who were the ones that handcuffed so many attendees as they were approaching the stage.

Finally, the need for all sorts of questions seemed superfluous. Tranquility, at last.

Jimmy grabbed him by the back of the collar and, turning to him, shouted incomprehensible sentences. Finally, with a worried look, he lowered him and leaned over, avoiding the accelerated crochet of one of the guys who were putting handcuffs. He lowered him completely and, before getting into the position to do anything, two hands got him sideways, grabbing him by the neck and shoulders. He fell.

Deceived by the blurred colorfulness of the view and the visible dots of mercurial colors that were part of it, Maximilian reached out to his friend. But the darkness swallowed him. The darkness was an invincible bully who finally took the opportunity to approach him from behind and melt the eyesight into his nothingness.

***

The walls of the wide corridors in front of the interrogation halls at the main police station were paved with honey-colored ceramic tiles in the shape of regular hexagons.

Maximilian had read long ago that such a hexagonal graphene layout, which the alchemists and Kabbalists regarded as a paradisiac and perfectly solid setting of the things in the Universe, was omnipresent as he himself was last night; one way or another, the snowflakes, the organic molecules, the testosterone and the heroin, the water and diamond crystals, the basalts, the bee hives, the epithelial eye cells, the soap bubbles... all were orderly structured in this pervasive hexagonal shape.

He was left lying in one of the chambers, left by a uniformed man with a mustache who said he would return.

Maximilian opened his left eye slowly and briefly, feeling a slight tingling sensation. Then the right one followed, slowly increasing the intervals of openness on both eyes.

The first thing he noticed were the same tiles which enclosed the space from the inside, too.

Six corners, just like the six days in which God created this imperfect and iniquitous world, but at the same time the first perfect number, according to the Pythagoreans.

He thought of his ever-present fear of this dreamy, mysterious number as a child. The visits of the kind and always smiling speech therapist.

Sometimes he thought it came from the church which was in the shape of two conjoined hexagons.

Approaching steps could be heard behind the massive metal door. After a quick while, a few low-pitched, alarming sounds coming from the lock distracted him and after the final unlocking sound, the door opened.

Maximilian, still lying on the ground, turned in the opposite direction from the high door through which two police officers stepped forward.

One of them was visibly older, had predominantly white hair and a mustache. The epaulettes were ornamented with an eight-pointed golden bordure and a golden star on the inside. Two gold-plated bracelets were embroidered on the side.

The junior officer's uniform, on the other hand, was adorned with only one star between two golden intertwined galloons. The only thing that really protruded was the perfectly trimmed black mustache which added a dozen years to his age.

The older one coughed.

Maximilian turned around, slowly adjusting himself to a sitting position, anticipating that he would lose his balance if he was even a tiny bit faster. Trying to gradually straighten his legs, he yawned.

"Good morning," he said.

The senior officer gave a signal to the younger one and the latter handed a piece of paper to Maximilian, who dreamily stared at it.

"The order for last night's search," said the senior police officer, "or the raid. I'll leave the choice of words to others."

Maximilian nodded, trying to read the note.

"I don't understand," he said.

"The reason, my boy, is that your friend Jimmy has already given us a reasonable suspicion that the event was going to lead to a large-scale abuse of narcotics."

Pressing his lips, Maximilian straightened his head and his body.

"What do you mean, officer?"

The older inspector smirked discerningly.

"We follow you, fellas. We have a whole team working on guys like you. And it's not only about your little band or your bunch of friends. We fear you guys could be a collateral victim of an internationally organized network, a vicious and heartless system involving dangerous drug traffickers from the region. We are talking about people from all walks of life: from regular slobs and rats, maybe around your age or a little older, to truly powerful string-pullers that determine destinies of the honest servants of this organized totality of people, like ours. "

"Do you refer to members of the government, inspector?"

The inspector laughed, stepping towards his interlocutor.

"Silly chap, we have no information about you, and a friend told us you aren't even part of the band."

"I'm not."

"Then, what the hell," the inspector frowned, "were you looking for in the filthiest hole on the planet with that hopeless riffraff that poisons the young, cultured, blooming, work-capable population?"

"I don't know."

"Did it really cross your mind that I might think you knew? Boy, at that age, if I knew what I was after in my life, I would've been pulling the strings by now."

The inspector took a pen out of his coat's inside pocket and, taking the note for a moment, called Maxim to sign it, placing the sheet on the nearby desk.

"Sign here," he said, pointing to the place for signature.

Maxim grabbed the pen, quickly scanned the minutes from start to finish, and in a matter of seconds his pupils became more than twice as wide.

With a sigh, the inspector raised his hand to throw a glance at his watch.

"Here you are," Maxim handed out the sheet.

The inspector's mobile phone rang with a ringtone playing unusually modern instrumental remix of *Habanera* from Bizet's *Carmen*.

"Yes? I understand," he said, putting the sheet back on the table.

"Excuse me for a moment," he said, quickly leaving the room.

Maxim's eyes seemed impatient with desire to find out what happened last night, inspecting every inch of the room in which not even the greatest mind exertion could make him remember how he ended up.

The young policeman's gaze was locked in a point, probably at the window with the monolithic canvas blinds that one could have expected them to remain in every second state institution since the previous regime.

The seriousness of his facial expression's seemed to camouflage his age, which Maxim assumed was roughly the same as his. Maybe he already had a family. It would be a bold-like idiosyncrasy for him to go clubbing, but he definitely had a good car.

Finishing the telephone conversation, the inspector got back.

"All right, thank you," he took the sheet again, "this was a small formal procedure that, alongside with a conversation with my colleague in the next room, is pretty much necessary for you to leave quickly and smoothly."

Maxim nodded.

"And what about my friends?"

"Your friends are waiting for the same procedure," the inspector met Maxim's eyes for a moment, "as soon as they wake up."

"Alright," Maxim said with relief.

"Actually, there is a small trifle with your cream of the crop playmate," the inspector added.

"What trifle?"

"Well... he'll have to rest for a day. Just one day and I believe he will do well. "

"Sir, Jimmy is completely innocent. He is..."

"I know he is, my child," the inspector interrupted, "the problem is not his innocence, but his extraordinary stupidity. And you know, we have a social and moral obligation to help young people heal from that addiction. "

Maxim slowly shifted his gaze to the left.

"Stupidity is a serious social problem, boy. But above all, a personal one marking out the sufferer. There's a lot of research that proves that, you know," the inspector raised an eyebrow. "Probably the best of the system solutions we could offer at this stage for your friend Jimmy's treatment is to provide him with appropriate conditions and therapy. The conditions are already known to you, and the therapy is not terrible at all. Just a few educational books. From start to finish."

"Will you... give Jimmy books to read?"

"I think it's fair, isn't it? Now... I hope he's not going to mind someone else choosing those books.

Maximilian smiled.

"Okay, boy, I'm leaving you to my younger colleague."

The inspector sourly lifted his left lip, revealing a tiny dimple in his plump cheek. He turned, preparing to leave.

"Sorry, I forgot to ask," he continued, returning, "what is your profession?"

The sourness poured slightly on Maxim's lips.

"An artist, sir."

"An artist?"

"Academic sculptor, officer."

"Academic sculptor?" He asked, turning his eyes to the

younger inspector. "I don't remember many academic sculptors going through this room... except for one, but he..." he giggled," he sculpted living people. And in the end, he got himself sculpted in jail. "

The inspector's phone rang again, so he pointed to the younger colleague and left the room.

Maximilian's gaze was focused on the lock that poured weird micro-cacophonic cocktails from high and low-frequency disharmonies into his ears.

That reminded him of something that was buried too deep for him to dare reach.

"Follow me," the young policeman said.

FREEDOM IS A DANCE OF THE SPIRIT AND THE BODY

It was Saturday. A cloudy afternoon. Maximilian was walking to the Grand Theater where a tragicomedy written by a famous playwright was to be premiered, with whom he had the honor of meeting a few summers ago.

He spent the previous few days in his apartment, trying to get some of his old life as a social butterfly back. Returning to the old social circle, he visited several exhibitions, performances, plays, musicals.

He once again allowed himself the opportunity to try his odds in dancing Latin dances with Alexandra, a colleague in doctoral studies at the Academy, a friend of the band and a bachata expert.

She had a slightly darker complexion than Maximilian, large black eyes, thick and emphasized eyebrows, full red lips, a round face and a toned, yet not over-muscular, body.

Step by step, freeing his mind and body until he learned the basics, Alexandra helped him relax at least for a moment.

He laughed again. His own mistakes were never funnier.

The girl had so much style and unreal sensuality in the movements with the dazzling tattooed legs and hips, shaped by the many years of cross-fit training.

She kept saying the body has absolute freedom. The dance of the body, she would say, only follows the mutual dance of the heart and the mind.

Maximilian's heart and mind slowly began to dance to the rhythm they set for themselves. But with the sculptor, things went in the opposite order, and he sought to develop that freedom of the mind and the heart through the freedom of the body.

Thus, freedom seemed to slowly become a principle.

Ha made an arrangement with Alexandra to go see the play and, noticing her in at the entrance, his smile naturally spread from ear to ear, so much that his upper lip almost touched the tip of his nose.

"You're late," she said, raising her eyes to Maxim's hairstyle.

"I knew I'd be."

"Why didn't you hurry then?"

"Why hurry when I already know I'm going to be late?"

"It's not a good sign for a girl to be waiting for you."

"I know that, too."

"You know a lot."

Maximilian shrugged indifferently.

The two entered and in a few minutes the play began.

***

Alexandra and Maximilian sat in the patisserie right across the theater, not far from the sea. It was run by an old Italian from the south.

"May I take your order, please?" The waiter said.

"For me, a Dacquoise and a blueberry juice," Alexandra said.

"And for you, Sir?"

"An île flottante, please."

"You mean a floating island?"

"Oui" Maxim answered," and some sweet liquor that goes with it."

"Which one?"

"Surprise me."

"Alright, it will only be a minute."

The table was metal, its legs were not perfectly equal, which Maxim found out after stretching out his leg towards Alexandra in an attempt to momentarily distract her from the smartphone, so he unintentionally kicked the longer leg making the table shake s. A newspaper, probably forgotten by a previous customer, fell down, and Maximilian picked it up.

"Be careful, young gent."

"Alright, young miss" Maximilian replied, caricaturing his voice as he opened the newspaper.

Alexandra continued tapping the smartphone. Maximilian drowsily went through the headlines in the various sections.

The waiter brought the desserts and the blueberry juice.

"Alexandra?"

"Yeah?"

"I know a really good neurosurgeon. My uncle's neighbor. "

"Mmm?"

"So you could implant the smartphone into your brain."

"They are calling me from work. I'll finish in a minute. "

"Yes, the body has absolute freedom. Yes, that's right. But the mind?" Maximilian wondered, leaving the newspaper open in the crime section, and after a minute, his phone rang.

"Jimmy?"

"What's up bro?"

"They freed you?"

"Like a bird. Like you are man... while you dance with that... Latino piranha."

Alexandra approached the cell phone.

"If you see her, say her hello from a hungry caiman who specialized in piranhas."

"He will... but she would also give you regards from a hungry South American jaguar who goes by the name Boyfriend" Alexandra shouted, grabbing Maximilian's hand, while returning to the newspaper with the other, reading an article in the crime section.

"So even the piranhas get boyfriends... for a day or two!"

"Well, when their natural enemies, the Caimans, disappear or, more precisely, get taken to the zoo, their movement is much freer and smoother."

"Someone ever told ya how badass of a girl you are, Alexa?"

"You mean as badass as a piranha that got swallowed by a caiman who thought it was all over until it got eaten from the inside?"

"Alright then, it is acknowledged, you're the biggest badass all the way to the Cayman Islands."

"Hey," Maximilian said, "when did they let you go?"

"Come to Ivana's garage tonight, you will find out everything."

"Okay, see you."

"Doll, this goes for you, too.'Til later."

Alexandra returned to her cell phone. The waiter printed the bill and with a quick step, he came to the table and gave it to them.

Maximilian closed the newspaper, staring blankly at the front page.

"This liquor" he said, "I don't know what this liquor is, but it gives the impression of madness saying it's the actual cure."

"It's great you've found pleasure in it without implanting that newspaper into your brain."

Maximilian sighed ironically.

"What's so interesting about that newspaper that you don't look away?"

"Take a look yourself" he raised the paper, pointing her glare at the cover page.

"What is it?"

"Ok, I'll read you the headlines:

Public administration employees announce general strike over mass layoffs weeks before the elections; Five movie-style robberies in a single day; Pomegranates - everything you need to know about this effective elixir and aphrodisiac; A serial killer lures for women - fact or detective fantasy?"

Mixed noises from a video game could be heard from Alexandra's mobile phone.

"You're committed to nonsense, my dear artist," she exclaimed.

"Unlike you, at least I'm committed. Let's go," Maxim said.

"Wait," she uttered enthusiastically.

"I'm gonna break that phone, I promise. I'll pay you, but I'll break it," said Maxim, pulling her by the arm, directing his step toward the wide promenade.

CONFESSIONS OF A POSSIBLE ONE-NESS

"Tunnel. Voices. Old. Young. Colorful. Unborn. Inhuman. Unheard of. Non-existent. Incomprehensible. You are incomprehensible.

Coldness. You run. The legs are running. The hands are flying. Your chest entraps all the worlds' clouds. The voices are becoming quiet, but their echo grows louder.

For a moment you think in a set voice. You fall into a pit. You are inside or vice versa. You stop thinking. The world you are a part of is completely alien to you. Darkness, in addition to being a representation of absence of light, is a consummate echo that resonates between the walls of your head. Your eye sockets are the channels through which the echo is released. Your connection to the outside world.

I feel afraid. There are only two or three, somewhat, familiar voices left. The echo overwhelms me. Only one voice left; the voice of the Heretic. It belongs to a famous person. I'm afraid to reveal his identity.

If I had a body, I would turn my head and run, loading each muscle to the limits of endurance. Or I would ride Artemio through seven mountains and valleys, seven rivers and woodlands, until I found the promised land of my bliss.

The voice puts my soul in tumult. It takes away my

whole freedom. It has chased me several times so far, even when I was awake. The last time it warned me; in fact, it conditioned me regarding the spy bird. I think I even saw him. He was a shadow. I fear of the end of this commanding demonic usurpation of my freedom; I'm afraid for me. He wants to reveal himself to me, either assuming I cannot recognize him, or to obliterate me.

But why would he need me?

I guess to keep me in fear and thus strengthen or maintain his dominance.

I approved his wish, and as hesitation is ripping my throbbing heart, I feel that I am regaining my body.

An unnatural heat covers my face, while the rest of my body is frozen by the cold. The voice belongs to the Poet.

The Poet and the Heretic seem like a whole, like two sides of the same coin. Maybe I am with them. I decide to try and establish some form of communication.

I ask the Heretic: *Are you a deity or just a shadow?*

Surprisingly, after a few moments, he answers through a question: *Isn't it the same?* It seems to me that, unlike the Poet, this time I am dealing with an immortal creature. Again, paralyzing my spirit and tying my body, the shadowlike archfiend haunts me every step of the way. The dance slowly turns from freedom into paralysis.

The adrenaline has too great liberty, which allows it to dance with other hormones smoothly; so much so that it threatens my own, mental liberty. The Heretic tells me again not to listen to my spirit or my body, and the rest of me obediently listens to him and only him. Being deprived by one's own body means that the recent emanation into His world is your only option.

Until the next, almost impatiently expected meeting with the same part of yourself,

M."

THE SKIES SHINING IN RED

Late in the evening, the already abandoned, yet still smoky, main room in the cabaret club was absolutely dominated by red walls and curtains. Someone had turned off the main lights.

Maximilian and Jimmy were sitting in the middle of the nine symmetrically placed high metal tables inside the empty club.

Robbie, smoking a cigar and accompanied by one of the waiters, was arranging the bar counter.

After a few moments, Mariana returned from the toilet and lit a cigarette.

The sensitive bloodshot eyes of the sleepless Maximilian blinked rapidly and instinctively, unable to bear the smoke.

"Guys," Jimmy said angrily, "this period for me is worse than your own lives."

"Why, Jimmy, sweetheart?" Mariana asked.

Leaning on the table, he turned down and, raising his feet, he directed his gaze to his boots.

"Crocodile skin. Italian."

"It's crocodile skin from Italy, Jimmy baby," Mariana smirked.

"My boots, sweetheart... I call 'em Italian 'cause they

look like Italy."

"Oh."

Jimmy grabbed a half-full bottle of whiskey from the middle of the table and poured it in the two glasses, bringing them closer to his interlocutors.

"Boots as boots. They always have something Italian. Leather, laces, threads, sole. The glue with which the sole is glued. Ah, even if it is not Italian goods, I guarantee the production manager or at least his deputy is Italian. Or the wife. Or fifty percent of their children. And the skin..." he extended his arm to his boots, "I envy the crocodile that was born in it", and he clenched his lips for a moment, then widened them.

"If it had been born in mine... it would've been as if he had seen a fish and swallowed a big shiny bait out of a toxic Chinese plastic." He put his hand in his pocket. "When it comes to crocodiles..." he pulled out a small transparent plastic sachet of pills, "the hungry caiman has not yet tried swimming in the waters of cannibalism."

Mariana and Maximilian observed him curiously.

"The hungry caiman has not yet tried swimming in the waters of cannibalism."

"What's that, tosspot?" Mariana approached the sachet.

"Hey," Jimmy frowned, "slowly, blondie! I know people like you can't do a thing when they need to understand something, but when their tongues release poisons near me, it can very easily poison them."

"What is that?"

"I'm a crocodile, I'll eat you if you're aggressive with me."

"What is it?"

"*Krokodil*. My product. Homemade elixir."

"What? Wait... what was that?"

"Desomorphine. Made from codeine, iodine and that red thing from the matchsticks. But yeah, I forgot you're a fucking blondie so you gotta ask questions about everything. "

"Cannibalism, huh?" Mariana kicked him.

Jimmy grabbed her leg defensively. "That's how it is,"

Robbie put aside one of the half-empty bottles that the waiter left on the bar counter.

"Hey, fugly!" he shouted, "did you know this shit can make your brain like that of a crocodile?"

"Oh, Mr. Boss!"

"Chill these meat-crumbling poisons and come help."

"If you don't want Mr. Boss to beat the fudge out of you!" Mariana added sarcastically.

"The thing about the meat-crumbling – that's partially a myth, invented by some silly ass cowards. I've tried it."

"Yup, it's obvious that you've tried crumbled meat," Robbie continued to raise the bottles at the counter.

"Oh my God! More and more dangerous things are becoming your toys, dude" Mariana said, "you're starting to scare me."

"You, too?"

"Just a bit more and you'll have to start with yourself," the surprised girl replied.

"Can't do it for a long time now," Jimmy said, "can't scare myself, darling. It looks as if that's scary enough... "

Maximilian put his hand on Jimmy's shoulder.

"Hey, what's gotten into you, man?!"

Jimmy exhaled with half-smile, suffocating the sound that was about to spontaneously come out, he unpacked the sachet and took out a pill.

The red side lights at the counter emphasized all the sharp lines on his face.

"Haven't tried this shit, have you?" He turned his head and his eyes from Mariana to Maximilian.

"What's wrong with you, Jimmy? We've known each other since we were little boys... I don't know you like this. These last couple of months, you've been..."

"People change, damn it," he put the pill in his mouth, taking another out of the sachet. He brought it closer to Maxim's face.

The waiter gave a gesticulating call sign to Mariana and

the next moment she found herself behind the counter surrounded by solvent cleaners.

"Look," Maxim hugged him, "you can tell me whatever you think is right, and you know I'd just..."

"...try to help and I know that if there was a chance, you'd succeed," Jimmy interrupted.

"You say there's no such chance?"

Jimmy raised his head with an artificial smile.

Maxim picked up the bottle of whiskey, tilted it, looking at each side, before finally stopping his eyes at the small letters of the declaration. *A thirty-five percent alcohol distillate with barley and honey. Shelf life: unlimited.*

"Oh, we're romantic!" Jimmy shouted. "Aren't we, by any chance, hungry, too?"

Maxim's pupils moved to the upper left corner for a moment before returning.

"Got enough crocodile food in here."

Maximilian, returning, glanced at Jimmy. Covering the lower lip with the upper, he tilted his head to the right.

"No, thanks."

"What's the matter with y'all? This is not that crocodile that breaks down human flesh."

"Man, how can you..."

"How can I what?! That's a pure form, you simpleton."

Jimmy took a glass left on the next table in his arms and started playing.

"Hey," Maxim approached him.

"What?" Jimmy answered as if surprised and with a questioning tone.

"I'm not a simpleton, pinhead," Maxim's eyes fixed on Jimmy's tight, static face.

"You're not?" Jimmy stood up, "then you have to be a self-deprecating clown who, because of the excessive harassment of his parents, the neighborhood childhood bullies who called him a *soldier* and the displeasure of the whole damn world, decided to create his own..." he slightly dropped the tone, "world… and to pathetically 'understand' himself as a misunderstood artist."

Maxim's hands slowly clenched, and in disbelief at what he heard, formed fists.

"But don't worry, I do understand you," Jimmy added, "I have an understanding of the misunderstood souls in our vast universe that's even larger than their own ideas."

Maxim's face was all of a sudden, nothing short of flushed, and his fists trembling.

Jimmy, leaning almost imperceptibly aside, left the glass he was playing with next to the open sachet.

A crooked artificial smile divided the lower part of his face into two. The elegance behind each movement of his fingers was calculated with extraordinary precision, at times reminding Maximilian of the articulation he achieved at full and absolute concentration while working on the most delicate segments of the new statue.

Suddenly, he stood in front of Jimmy. Raising his right hand, he grabbed him by the neck, pushing him off with the other hand.

Jimmy burst into a frenzy, barely reciprocating in a failed attempt to grab the sachet. Waving his hands, he pushed the table, and the clang of the glass was heard, followed by an even more air-piercing shattering of the whiskey bottle. The pills were scattered between the several pools from the liquid on the floor and the dry area.

Maxim tried to capture his arms.

"What are you two cretins doing?!" Robbie got up almost simultaneously with the waiter and Mariana, who walked up to the two of them.

Maxim, making few vigorous movements, almost succeeded to capture Jimmy, who was still wandering chaotically. In an instant, Maxim managed to strike Jimmy's nose with the left elbow, than he grabbed him by the leg, but Robbie, who was behind him at the time, and the waiter, who just got by to stand between the two, prevented him from hitting him,.

"Now both of you madmen, get the hell out of my bar!" Robbie shouted.

It was not particularly difficult to separate the angry boys. The corpulent waiter managed that in a moment.

Mariana, shouting, also stood behind Maxim, pulling him by the waist.

"What on Earth made you try to prove yourself to that mock jester!?" she addressed him in a disturbed manner.

The stunned Maxim was too focused on his opponent to respond.

"Oh, you zany, you're worse!"

Maxim turned angrily to her.

"If I'm worse, get your shit outta here and don't show your face to me! Understand?"

Maxim separated from the others and, shaking off and adjusting his shirt, stepped towards the exit.

"Wacko wazzock," Jimmy shouted, "even if you sell your soul and all the stupid sculptures to the fucking devil, you won't collect enough for the white junk you just destroyed! You numskull..."

Maxim took the deepest breath possible and left the cabaret club briskly.

The outer carotid artery protruded from the left side of his neck.

Gradually accelerating, he did not look away, staring at the horizon with greenery and candelabra at the street's end, while the Sun enveloped the whole sky with its rarely sumptuous sunrise, magnanimously gleaming its red glow, similar to Maxim's bloody eyes.

It was quiet. No taxis, no cars, no buses or trams. Just a distant and familiar barking of a street dog.

Riding a bike from the back, an inconspicuous girl, after coming out of a narrow passage, turned her head slightly and did not move, so that the clumsy Maxim almost got hit in the groin by her steering wheel.

He turned impulsively, shouting for more than half a

minute.

The voiceless girl frowned, muttered a few incomprehensible sentences and continued.

Maxim kept shouting, gradually lowering his tone.

His left carotid artery was more visible than ever. He bent, covering the face with his palms. Stayed a few moments like that - only himself and his breath.

The pricking sensation under the upper eyelids indicated tears of restlessness and anger, but it was interrupted by a sudden attention refocusing on the touch of his left shoulder. Gentle and absorbent. Even his instinct recognized Mariana's palm.

"Let's go. The day is about to come."

He felt the trembling of the lacrimal glands between his eyes, whose red glow lustered brighter and brighter from the rising Sun.

BOTTOMLESS, FATHOMLESS RED DOTS

"I do not know how many more nights the Heretic i.e. the Poet thinks he will be able to divert my attention from the Muse. He seems to be an inhuman and immortal creature, alien to my limited worldviews and thoughts, just as they were to others while he was alive. Yes, he is a transcendent being immanent to my will while I sleep. And that is it. I have to face the fact of his immanent intrusion.

I have to do my best to make it clear that my will is determined strictly by my opinion.

The fact that my muse has put me in the 'ignore zone' for quite some time now gives an additional momentum of unrest to my soul which arises from his control over my visualization and overall cognition.

I will have to prove to her that behind my artistic pride lies nothing short of a preeminent creative prowess - the result of her incredibly real presence, materialized again and again in every fraction of my chef d'oeuvre.

Maybe that bewitching bane, an embodied curse, is just envious that the sculptures are not hers, as is probably the case with her not belonging to her own self.

On several occasions, I have had different thoughts about her relationship with the Heretic. Maybe she is another of his works?

And why not, given the power it has over my ill spirit and the dazzle over the ability to see clearly and distinctly. She is, now I can confidently say, a hallucination, a clouding of my mind occurring, I believe, in precisely defined situations. I will study the details of the circumstances in which this dimness occurs.

In any case, the hallucination or eidolon I am experiencing, and with which I have agreed to be my Muse, obviously deviates from its part of the agreement.

I do not even want to think that the intrusion of all those destructive and so vivid lines of images indicate any further step by my mind's usurper. Of course, I have in mind that whenever they appear, they are neither more nor less than pure mental representations, no matter how much they want to be picturesque and vivid.

Given this fact, I do not feel a particular need to share their content.

I hope they will soon begin to leave me, along with other mental phenomena that make me feel terribly hopeless, forcing me to shut myself up.

I wish I had the opportunity to gather strength to express all this to the Heretic, but he has absolute telepathic control over me whenever he wants, and that makes Katya just a toy or an additional tool for even more sophisticated intrusion and control in my real world, of which I am getting more and more tired to write about.

I would talk, but I am afraid, in fact, I am panicking that if I reveal this to Dr. Andrea or any other medical person, my hospitalization would be a matter of time.

That would tear my already depleted by the constant insomnia mental strength to pieces as small as the pieces of paper will be as soon as I finish this diary entry.

Unfortunately, that uptight twit Jimmy, my oldest

friend, in the onslaught of his neurotic and frustrated outbursts, making a projection of his own experience, somehow got some things right about my childhood.

Sometimes I think the hopeless bud knows me better than I do.

Yes, any imprisonment in a mental institution would kill me, and if it doesn't, I would.

On the other hand, if I were to face the omnipotent and seemingly inexhaustible source of Evil in my subconscious, I would become a far better, stronger, and more independent version of myself than any therapy could ever help me become. My madness is probably the secret weapon with which I manage to reach the sublimity and elegance of the Art for which the one who inspires, kills and resurrects me on a daily basis, preaches and because of which some declare me a narcissistic and self-absorbed fanatic.

Jimmy simply swallows the frog that runs away from the swamp where we are all drowning, thinking it could make him a crocodile.

An extremely talented, but angry fellow. A Millennial Narcissus who has yet to delve into his own depths before exiting to the other side and noticing his reflection on what gives him the impression of pure water.

After all, being a musician and having a well-developed sense of hearing is nothing but a reflection of his childhood traumas. I remember his father screaming every day, locking Jimmy and his sick mother in the bathroom, while we, the kids from the neighborhood, stood in amazement under his window, listening intently to the cries that were the inspiration for so many hood jokes, allowing us to come up with the wickedest of his nicknames: *Bidet.*

And he, although ruthlessly, taught Jimmy to fight against necessity and also against the weaker, telling all of us once again that everything is a struggle and that death is the only way to stop it.

Mariana thinks that Jimmy had a new problem with his

father. She concluded this based on examples from the past –
whenever he was in messy situations at home, his desire for vio-
lence and escape from reality always went through the roof.

I am going to pay him a visit, even if I am forced to wipe
the floor with his plumpy ass.

In anticipation of bringing about a new self-evolution,
M."

***

The day shone lavishly, attacking with its intense light
the corneas which were about to meet halfway.

March looked like a confused little boy at a crossroads or
an insecure football player who unconsciously commits himself to listen only to the voice of the audience.

Maximilian had just finished an essential segment of the
new sculpture.

Working with superhuman effort, he hurried to bring the
day through the senses which the Sun was helping him open.

Thoughts slowly turned into joy after the fruitful endeavor.

Delight. Freedom paving the way for rampancy, with his
mind as clear as the sky.

After a month of intensive work, he decided to try a form
of meditation in his favorite place in the park.

The road to the park led to Dr. Andrea's office.

The street was empty.

"It looks like these kids have found a more interesting
pastime," Maximilian thought in anticipation of the usual children's noise as he passed by.

A blonde girl holding a plastic folder case came out of the
doctor's office.

The sculptor noticed her and at the moment when her
gaze seemed utterly ready to meet his, he got out of the sidewalk and continued with expedited pace.

Soon he found himself in the middle of the glowing

greenery of the park surrounded by young people celebrating the day with a picnic.

After the meditation, he got up.

The chlorophyll penetrating through every pore inspired him to stay.

However, the day was predestined for many other things.

Leaving the park, he got into one of the taxi cabs parked at the side of the narrow cobbled street.

"Moscow St., number twenty-four," he told the taxi driver, relaxing his back while holding the back of his head with his elbows pointed sideways, and sniffling loudly with his nose.

"Sorry, I really revel in this smell... a smell of brand new," he added.

"That's because the car is brand new, and so is the freshener," the taxi driver replied, pointing to the tiny cylindrical box above the radio with the same color as the grass from a while ago.

The yellow car was slowly passing the alleys connected to the main road leading to Moscow St.

After a short time, it stood in front of a high gate with sharp wrought iron tops and Maxim came out.

The gate was closed, but Maxim knew there was a hidden metal knob on the inside that could serve as a gate opener by moving it to the left.

Maxim opened and carefully closed the gate, eagerly rushing to Jimmy's house where strange noises could be heard from the back, some kind of buzzing.

As if they came from a machine, probably a drill.

Maybe Jimmy was repairing the garage, as he once proclaimed he would.

Maxim turned to the right, taking a semicircular walk around the house. Jimmy was in front of the open garage holding a large cobalt drill in his hands, whirring into the empty space. He was sitting on a barrel with his back turned to Maxim and he could not notice his arrival. It seemed as if he was testing the device.

For a moment, he turned off the machine, making the humming stop, then raised his head and took a deep breath.

Maxim, raising his eyebrows, tiptoed slightly changing the angle of his approaching.

A spiky object was attached to the thick tip of the metal rod.

Maxim, standing a few steps away, hesitantly touched his beard.

Jimmy lowered his head, pressing the button that caused the 800 watt machine to double its operation.

Maxim approached stealthily, stopping just three or four steps behind Jimmy, who raised the machine and quickly turned it towards himself. In a spur, he pulled it a foot away and pulled hard toward himself, aiming at his own heart.

At the same time, Maxim jumped over him, grabbing the powerful machine.

"What the hell is wrong with you, dumbass?!" he shouted, punching him hard in the biceps.

The drill bit had only barely pierced the shirt, leaving a red dot. Jimmy tried to retaliate with a clumsy half-punch from the left, but Maxim grabbed both of his hands, while tripping him with the right leg.

His friend collapsed with immutable clumsiness, dropping the massive tool on the ground.

He smelled of alcohol. And indeed, there was a bottle of homemade brandy next to the garage wall.

Maxim lifted the drill, pointing it at the sky. An iron figure of a white king with a sharp crown from the chess he received as a birthday present from Mariana was glued to the cobalt top.

"You didn't answer my question, dumbass," Maxim kicked his supine, ragged friend in the butt, who instead of answering, nervously let out a deep, threatening sound.

"Did you really want to insert a metal chess king in your heart?"

"You're not the only one who's got the chess in his heart."

"A serious potential for being ass-whooped lies in that heart of yours."

Taking the metal figure off the drill, Maxim kneeled.

"C'mon, explain it to me" he said, "what the fuck's going on. Get up" he held out his hand.

Jimmy got up on his own, and Maxim found himself behind him for a moment, helping Jimmy stay on his feet. He went to the wall, where he left the drill in exchange for the unopened bottle of brandy, listening to short and abrupt exhalations.

He turned. The man whom he had considered his sincerest well-wisher and partner in crime was crying. The red spot, visibly enlarged, already covered about a third of the front of the shirt.

"Damn," he said, halting his intention to pour alcohol on his wound, "come."

The half-drunk, stifled from his sobbing Jimmy, welcomed his best buddy with open arms, looking like a lost child in the middle of a crossroad. His cheeks flushed and his face glowed.

Maxim felt a flow of energy through his stomach that gave him a mélange of feelings of immense anguish woven with islands of relieving solace.

"Can't do that, Max" his pal said through tears.

"What, Jimmy?"

"I just can't."

"What can't you do?"

"Kill him."

Maxim tried to hide his startled gaze by shifting the attention towards the wound that was becoming more and more obvious and sight-consuming.

"Wait, I'll clean your wound. Take the shirt off."

Jimmy turned his head down as he unbuttoned his cotton shirt. In a few moments he finished unbuttoning and handed the shirt to Maxim, who bent the bottle over his chest.

"This is going to hurt. Ready?"

As if giving a sign of approval, Jimmy blinked, and the next moment Maxim started pouring the liquid over the wound. Jimmy's facial expression remained unaffected. His friend rolled up his shirt, improvising a bandage that he dipped in the brandy. He wrapped the wound, placing the cloth-bandage between the right side of his neck and the space under the ribs on the opposite side, squeezing it hard from behind.

"I can't, Maxim."

"What is it that you can't, dude? What kind of murder are you talking about?!" The artist lowered the half-empty bottle.

"He... he..." he burst into tears again.

"Hey," Maxim grabbed his head, "take it easy. I am here. Your pal Max is here."

Jimmy nodded, staring at an indefinite point.

"Who is he? Who do you want to kill?"

"My... my old man."

Maxim pulled his head back with a confused grimace.

"Your father?"

Jimmy lowered his head, hiding it with his palm.

"He... he fucked Matthew. He raped... my son."

Maxim's neck, which did not know how to express his disbelief in what he was hearing, instinctively transfixed.

"What?"

Until that moment, Jimmy's tears seemed inexhaustible. In his failed attempt to free them once more, he turned to the garage, matching his direction with that of the unoperating drill.

THE KIDNAPPED REVERIES OF BUOYANCY

The leather armchair meant for clients in Dr. Andrea's office was exceptionally soft and soothing. Maxim sat with his hands in his pockets, laid-back and serene.

"When did such dreams first occur?" The doctor interrupted the silence, drawing some irregular geometric shapes on the yellow paper of her notebook.

"It's hard to be precise, but I will say that a little less than a year has passed since then," Maxim replied.

"Nine? Ten months?"

"About ten."

Leaning her head against her folded arms, the doctor gazed thoughtfully behind her co-talker into the library's upper right corner loaded with red books.

"And do you remember when the first letter from the Heretic came to you?" she asked.

"It happened the same time as the first dream."

"And how many letters have you received?"

"Three."

The doctor rested her temple on her index finger.

"What are they all about?"

"Intimate things, doctor."

"Of what kind?"

"I don't know if I would like to open up that much so early, to be honest. But I would like to convey to you my premonition that something is wrong with them. "

"Okay, in what manner?"

"It's as if they reveal some things about me. Hidden, deeply buried features and events that I don't know if I myself..." Maxim whispered, "would like to know. With each following letter, it's as if things that I have done or witnessed are being revealed to me without being... aware."

The door to the room suddenly opened and Maxim got up to close it again.

"Well, that is a bit unusual."

"Exactly, doctor, which is why I'm concerned and addressing you."

"And what do you do after a letter arrives?"

"Write down its content, as well as my thoughts, actions and plans in a diary."

"Hmm... tell me... how do you think that oxymoronic Divine Heretic would react after learning about our little conversation?"

"Well, I do not know."

"When one does not know, one usually assumes..." the doctor pointed her hand at Maxim with her palm in a gesture attempting to prompt his response.

The sound of playing with a ball and children's shouts came from the window. Several leaves from unknown trees, circularly wind-blown, could also be seen.

"May I guess?" The doctor added.

"Sure."

"I will guess, but first you have to admit that you felt slightly scared a while ago."

"When you asked me?"

"Yes."

"Maybe. But more like, super-slightly."

"And just maybe a bit more, although it is a question of whether you are fully aware of it."

Dr. Andrea got up and went to the cupboard, took a bottle of already prepared gin fizz and two glasses and put them on the desk.

"Is that a blueberry gin fizz?"

As a sign of hesitation, Maxim dropped a softly tinted *m* through his nose.

"You don't have to if you don't want to."

"But I do. Please."

The doctor filled the square glasses, handed one to him, and picked up hers for a toast.

"Have you ever met someone who reminds you of the appearance of that man? It can be in anything – his appearance, face, proportions, voice, tone, movements?"

"Yes, a poet."

"A poet?"

"His name was Charles. It seems to me that... in fact, I'm quite convinced that the heretic is only... only his immortal form from the afterlife."

"So that poet of yours, Charles, is dead."

"Yeah, he was an alcoholic who died writing his greatest work or, Magnum Opus. Doctor, maybe... "

"M?"

"Maybe all this is a completion of his work. Sort of."

"Could be," Andrea nodded, "in which case, you are the one 'he' wants to make it happen."

"I thought so, too," Maxim said, drinking from the glass.

"And how would you describe Charles' character?"

Maxim looked up, staring at the Venetian blinds that reminded him of his home.

"Well... in few words, he was an irreconcilable rebel unbothered by his age to remain a zealous fighter for his ideals."

"So rather energetic and impulsive than calm and sober?"

"Ha-ha, doctor," Maxim laughed, "I couldn't imagine Charles calm and sober even in the ninth circle of Paradise, especially sober."

"Empyrean."

"Excuse me?"

"Dante would say that the ninth circle of Paradise is the so-called Empyrean."

Maxim lowered his gaze, noticing the play of two children with a ball in the middle of the street through the not-so-lowered blinds.

"Tell me, Maxim, or Maximillian... Did Charles' behavior at times seem inconsistent to you? Did he ever..." the doctor recalled, "reveal any of his private problems to you? Some of those from his darkest hour?"

"The word *problem* itself is the shortest life description of that weirdo."

"Could you recall a specific one he confessed or complained about?"

"It was a daily occurrence," Maxim said, "he was constantly complaining about the women from the past, the injustices that society thrusted upon his brother, the destitution..."

"So he had a brother?"

"Yes, but he died very early."

"I see," the doctor said, taking a cigarette out of the wide metal cigarette case on the desk.

"Do you smoke?" she offered one.

"No, thank you."

Andrea lit a cigarette.

"So? The answer to my first question would be...?"

Maxim smiled mildly and asymmetrically.

"I forgot, I'm sorry."

"About the inconsistency in the behavior of your friend-poet. Maybe I should clarify – have you ever thought he behaved in contrastive ways, had sensibly different emotional reactions in the same or similar situations?"

"Like mood swings?"

"More about worldviews poles apart. Now, that also includes mood discrepancies. Something like two or more different personas instead of just one."

"When I think of it, yes, many times. After all, the poet's worldview was poles apart from that of the Heretic. While the former told me that the world did not deserve my energy and passion to change for the better, the Heretic, addressing me with a peculiar, sacred name that begins with the letter E, continues to tell me that the struggle for a better world is the majestic mission of my corporeal existence."

"An interesting set of words. And tell me, but please, very honestly... have you noticed such changes, discrepancies in yourself?"

Maxim leaned his forehead with his index finger.

"Yes, doctor. After all, the reason I address you - my hallucinations - I always experience them differently and that makes me react in diverse ways, making me look like a different person, kind of a touch-and-go inclination."

"It is fascinating that you have brought yourself to this level of awareness. But one thing is not clear to me: why, on earth, did you not seek help immediately? You do not help anyone by doing nothing, young man."

"I know, but..."

"Were you scared?"

Making an awkwardly stiff expression with his lips and the lower part of his cheekbones, Maxim bowed his head.

"That unbelievable rebellious fear – can sometimes be a source of divine power. Unfortunately, at times it can confront you with something else. Maxim, now maybe you really do have a reason to be afraid, to consider..."

"Will the heretic return?"

"No one can know that," she said, opening a drawer in the middle of the desk.

She took out a prescription and a stamp and started writing. He finally hit the press, handing the paper to the young artist.

"Here it is."

"What is this?"

"Your remedy."

Maxim struggled to read the names of the drugs.

"Ol-an-za-pine. A-ri-pi-pra-zole."

"You will use them according to the instructions."

Maxim nodded.

"Tell me, do you have a family?"

"Yes, but we have very little contact."

"And why is that?"

"I don't know. Probably because of my mother. My papa had a stroke a few years ago and remained immobile."

"And what about your mother? Bad memories?

"It's hard for me to be close to her."

"I think this is the case with many young men," Andrea looked at her watch. "Well, I will be seeing you again in three days. Then we will have more time to share and get to know some things about your life, including the relationship with your parents. And please, send me a message when you get the prescribed doses of olanzapine and aripiprazole."

"Alright, doctor."

On the other side of the reopened door that had a faulty lock, a young blonde doctor's assistant appeared.

"This way, please," she pointed to the exit.

***

The midnight was separated by a few insignificant minutes from the moment when the thunderous techno from the largest club on the outskirts of the city had just begun to resonate, touching the atelier with halved force.

The artist closed the windows and tiredly collapsed on his bed.

His eyes were meagre, spontaneously tearing, and he reached for the pills left on the bedside table, quickly swallowed them with the help of the still hot and barely drinkable mint tea.

Leaving the half-empty glass, he crawled back in bed

and, crossing his legs in a semi-meditative position, absent-mindedly fell asleep.

He felt as if entering a portal in the shape of a semicircular mirror, pointing in a somewhat familiar direction. For a moment he found himself standing in the middle of a floating platform or island of massive stone blocks. The super-strong gravity was tenaciously gripping his body and the air was humid and foggy, not allowing the vertical or horizontal end of the huge space to be seen. Judging by the sounds, water seemed to be flowing under the platform.

Somewhere roughly in the center of the platform that resembled a rhomboid, a regular hexagon was drawn with Maximilian standing in the center.

Suddenly, a thunderous baritone could be heard, followed by an echo.

"Welcome," the voice said.

The fog over the artist began to thicken, creating a vortex, which gradually began to take on the colors and shapes of a winged human silhouette. In a few moments the vortex descended before Maximilian, materializing itself in a human figure with assembled white wings and a face reminiscent of the Poet.

"I have heard that you are afraid of me," the figure declared without moving his already blurred lips.

Maximilian was motionless, knowing he was asleep.

"Of me? Or maybe... of yourself?" The figure walked in a semicircle around Maximilian, "of the imperfection you embody with your own art and actions? Of the awareness of the distance from your mission's ultimate goal? Of the fear that, in the search for your own wings and perfection, like me standing here pure and impeccable in my deeds, without vices and wheelchairs. Dear Enoch, faith means death to fear. Only faith could help you sacrifice all the habits and sinful thoughts that have brought you here."

The color of the whole room changed into a mixture of green and grayscale-dark red shades in just a few moments.

Fighting against gravity, Maximilian first managed to make a few micro-movements, and then to make a step, directing his torso to the nearest edge of the floating rhomboid island after leaving the hexagon. He was one step away from the abyss. The figure finally stopped.

"You know everything, Enoch. It is no coincidence that you grew up in a house of worship, and you know that. But the one whose absurd help consists of drugs should bring you back on the path of the supposed serenity and supremacy of reason, surely does not know it. The kenosis is not far away, but you will have to get closer to God. To climb the mountains behind the ocean of knowledge and proficiency in which you will soak your pen as soon as you become, as soon as you return to your original form - Metatron. Because you are the brightest and closest angel to God, Enoch. You cannot be afraid of yourself, of your own light. There is light in front of every shadow, and in front of yours is His, which is ever-present in You. Be with yourself."

The figure looked up and the room turned sky blue.

"If you don't fight, you don't have the right to be surprised when you see others doing it. Including your doctor."

"No! She is not involved in the Plan. Andrea can and will help me. "

"Her medications may be able to treat people, Enoch. But not angels."

The modified figure turned to Maximilian in an instant. The front of the head now had a face with variable shapes. The cheeks, the eyes, the nose, the lips, the chin, and the cheeks transformed over time, giving the impression of him having multiple faces.

The next moment he rose, he dematerialized his perfect body to the heights ending in a white mist.

In the quiet, cheerful spring night, Maxim's body inadvertently hugged the thin cotton blanket from the bed.

Turning to the left, with his bare knees, since the very moment of awakening, he had clenched his round velvet pillow.

The last raindrops could be heard outside.

After getting up and quickly changing his clothes, he stopped for a few moments, to take a look at the statues, and all four, set in the four corners of the atelier, looked like they had just left the world.

He watched them abstracting himself from the sense of time. As an artist of visuals, he was surprised to find that once again, after a while, he was consumed by the simple sight of objects in a stainless perfection.

He approached them.

Eros breathed the rapturous ardor of the world which borders seemed breathless from long ago.

He may have been blown away by the still unfinished Storge, whose breasts had yet to take their detailed, planned shape.

He was breathing love. Approaching the statue at a distance of less than two feet, he slowly moved his palms towards her shoulder. The tips of her fingers, radiating desire, crawled on their own, as if they wanted to dig out one another, just for her sake, just for a moment, the world's inmost mysteries.

His pupils were comfortably buried under the safety cloak of his eyelids, which separated him from everything he knew would deprive him of the concentration he needed for Oneness.

And yet he opened them.

He had to see the way to the realization of the idea which only disturbed his peace for a moment. Going to bed, he took the medicine boxes and took out the colorful tablets one by one, placing them in his left palm. Then he returned to the statue of Storge.

Behind the statue was a wooden stack of clay, navel height, and to the right on the floor there was a bucket of water.

He stood in front of the stand and took a piece of clay with his right hand, dipped it in the bucket several times, waiting for it to soften, and pressed it hard several times, flattening it. Squeezing the tablets from the inside, he forcibly bent the piece of clay and covered them from all sides.

The rain had long gone, leaving behind a rainbow visible through the window right in front of the sculptor's eyes, whose natural joy seemed colored in billion colors, more than those of the tablets.

The unfinished Storge had a huge gap, a hole in the middle of the front of the torso and the abdomen. Not even her legs were finished, but Maximilian was convinced that he would succeed, in fact, he wanted to focus his efforts much more on her breasts, to make them more consummately precise than any sculptor ever could.

Holding the piece of clay, he began rubbing it alternately with his palms, getting a circular, slightly elongated, slightly spindle-shaped contour which was extended at the top.

He approached the statue with a smile and pushed it hard into the center of the cavity where the breasts were to be.

"Your heart does not need medicine. Storge's heart is a medicine in itself," he said to himself, pushing hard.

Forgetting the exterior, in a few minutes he entered the usual creative drive.

The moment of thought for the initial breast-shaping strategy was instantly interrupted by a well-known female voice:

"You know you're unable to do it without me."

The artist stopped working and, smirking, with his head down, bit his upper lip.

"What made you reappear?"

"I did not leave. I was abducted."

"By whom?"

"By those who are trying to steal your pleasure from the Oneness with your own art only because they have never experienced anything similar."

"You are lying. Last time, you identified me with a mythical character intoxicated with his own reflection."

"Narcissus?" Katya laughed. "He is the embodiment of the divine Art. The divine in nature that aspires to be art."

"He sank into the water and drowned."

"He had the courage unavailable to other mortals to appreciate his own equality and oneness with the angry gods who drowned him. But in that infinitely short moment of self-knowledge, his divinity was equated with the only and highest Joy, hitherto known only to those beyond."

Maximilian opened his eyes and turned in a circle. She was gone.

"If you live the Joy yourself, don't ask where I am. Come and save me."

The voice left.

Maxim briskly took off his shoes, took the leather backpack left next to Eros's sculpture and left the studio.

He passed through the main square and sat on a bench behind the mall, borrowed a cigarette from a passer-by and at the same moment on the pole to the opposite noticed a sticker with a photo of a familiar person.

"And... Andrea?", Touching his nape, he rolled his eyes, a moment before he caught sight of a point at half the height at which the sticker was placed.

***

Mariana, Jimmy, Sylvester, Philip, and Simon the bassist, all sat on the elevated cement steps in front of the main skate park, watching the training of the twenty-something young skaters, which was consisted of competitive executions of particular pirouettes.

At times, some of the boys stopped for a breath or for concentration before continuing to the next step. Mariana's gaze on one of the jumpers was equally focused as the skaters'.

At one point, one of the teenagers fell down clumsily, tearing his stretchy jeans at his right knee, and three of those present rushed to help him get up.

"Does anyone have an idea where, the fuck, is Alexandra? I haven't seen her since that night... " said Simon.

Jimmy was sitting with his head down, holding his knees.

"Guys," he said, exhaling loudly, "weird things happen, haven't you noticed?"

Simon got up, lazily stretching.

"We're too weird to notice anything," Philip said.

"What weird things, Jimmy?" Mariana asked.

"I haven't seen Alexandra either. Nor have her parents. And by God... not even the police. "

"What?" Mariana asked, glancing at Jimmy, "is there a police search for her?"

"Yes, from few days ago."

"Are you serious?"

"Both her parents and the police thought I might know something about it, so they called me for an informative conversation."

"And?"

"I told them I heard about the whole thing from them. Haven't seen her since my last hobnob with the police either. I don't know why, but even that was strange to them."

"Maybe they thought you gave her some experimental chemistry?" The blonde asked in a cunning tone.

"Ha-ha..." remarked Jimmy half-ironically, closing his lips abruptly.

"You mean before she starts stealing our experimental chemistry?" Simon asked.

"So? Do you know anything about her disappearance, Jimmy?"

"No, Mariana," Jimmy said, "if I knew anything about my top fan, I would be the first to share."

"I hope so."

"Hey, guys," Sylvester said, "do you think it could be related to..."

"The disappearance of the girl from the cabaret club?" Simon added.

"We don't know if there was actual disappearance from

the cabaret club," Jimmy said in an almost resenting tone. "What the police know is that the girl was spotted there for the last time, and that's actually the main reason they kept me at the station back then."

"Do you know the missing girl?" Mariana wondered.

Slightly smiling, Jimmy let out a sigh of relief under his mustache.

"Anna. She was my ex..."

Simon laughed.

"Yup, that's her name," Silvester added.

"An alluring, memorable girl. In the morning she had those bright green eyes that became a little darker at night. Intelligent, open-minded, positive, bold, and, very often, a risk-taker. Don't want to chase patterns, but she was a redhead too."

"What did the police say?" Mariana asked.

"They interrogated me about the last time we saw each other, whether I could point out people she was seeing, then they examined my relationship..."

"Do they know anything specific?"

"I don't think so. They mentioned she was the third twenty-something girl to go missing in a similar way in a period of few months."

"What do they mean similar way?"

"I don't know. They didn't seem very much assured. They obviously don't have a clue if it's an organized network or something else."

"That's some bizarre shit right there," said Simon. "First, your ex with whom the band spent the evening, literally in the same bar, then a girl who's a top fan of the same band in the midst of an album promotion. I don't know what the eyes of those inspectors are made of, Jim, but make sure they don't wear any sniper glasses."

Sylvester opened his backpack and pulled out a newspaper.

"And here it is, cronies," he said, pointing to the front page of the newspaper.

The headline read: *Three girls missing in less than a year.*

Under the headline, written in bold: "The police do not rule out a connection, the dilemma is whether if it is an organized network, a group, an individual or something else. Details of the investigation have not yet been released and they have announced that they will issue a statement on the case soon. In today's issue of *The Informer*, we bring you conversations with relatives and friends of the missing persons."

While each of them read the caption, Sylvester observed their faces with a subdued half-smile.

"And what did they tell Maxim at the station?" Mariana asked, passing quickly through the rows.

"I don't know, we haven't really talked about it."

The gazes of Simon and Sylvester flashed occasionally through the park, noticing the unusual and wacky maneuvers of the young skaters.

"And here it is," Mariana pointed out, "one of the investigators in charge of the investigation says there is an obvious link between the profiles of the missing girls, but in the interest of the investigation's progress, he will keep any further details undisclosed" she successively lowered and elevated her bright eyes.

CREATION NO. 4

Storge's breasts slowly took the intended shape as her creator's hands slowly and skillfully manipulated the hard clay and then the ceramic womb from where bronze art was to be born.

When this occurred, the inconspicuous difference in size was lost in the obscure tendency to symmetry and regularity, despite the apparent difference in shape, while the nipples swelled proudly in the sacred centers of their impeccable ovality as crowns of a glorious existence.

The calculated and playful feats of the sculptor in their deft uplift over the rest of the torso, built a material order of chaos, the meaning of which was more and more certain in Maximilian's eyes to play with and between the seemingly contrasting modalities of the beautiful and the sublime.

"The one is as smooth and angular as its sweet-tasting irises," the sculptor said in silence, "while the other is the hoarse volcano that swallows desires and eavesdrops on them in the form of transcendental passions when we are One, dear."

The statue listened.

It was by listening to his kenotic screams in the moments of creation that she animated the Oneness itself.

They, similar to bodily lips in the midst of a body crucified in the air, seemed to express their dreams to him loudly, no longer afraid of the demons guarding the silence.

Storge listened and wanted to be heard like any true friend.

The friendship with Storge for Maximilian meant coalescing with the silences; those from outside; those inside. The deepest. The unstoppable. He knew they existed.

He cummed.

Tears welled up in his eyes, appearing like oval microgleams of light, the mini suns moving elegantly as his hands, as if seeking a common artistic purpose at the end of the movements.

The touch with the soil seemed to be a touch between the canvas and the color drops that seek their purpose in the final realization, seemingly purely expressionist; however, the expression and the impression were touched, and apart from Maximilian, his extraordinarily finished creation also knew that unconditionally.

The touches embodied in the lush, sensual, accentuated breasts of Storge were touches of various meats and souls, beautiful and sublime, who, longing for each other, recreated each other as if they were sculptors themselves.

Maximilian's hands relaxed with the artist's last sigh.

At that moment, he closed his eyes and the bell rang.

As if it was called to interrupt the beginning of a self-becoming contemplation and restorative quiescence.

"I'm coming!" said the sculptor loudly, taking a wet cloth to wipe his hands.

Someone was impatient. The bell rang again and a moment later there was a knock at the door. Maxim lowered the cloth, came to the door, turned the key and opened it.

"Good day Sir, we are inspector Peter Chingo and inspector Dushan Solovetsky, officers from the main police station in Marckest."

Maxim looked at the two uniformed men in confusion.

"May we?" Inspector Peter pointed with his palm inward.

"Yes, of course. Welcome." the sculptor opened the door with the lower part of his left palm, watching out for a few unshaven smaller spots. The police officers entered.

"I have always been fascinated by the smell of artwork spaces," inspector Dushan commented, taking a deep breath.

"It's gotten too deep into me," Peter added, "painting was my father's great, impassioned hobby," he said, looking at Maxim.

"Your father was a great painter. It was really original of him to paint only in blue and he was still able to capture a whole philosophy in every detail. "

"You are wrong. The blue dominated his paintings before the collapse of our former country. After its breaking apart, he painted only in red."

"Well, then..."

"Excuse me, officers," Maxim interrupted, "I'll go to the bathroom for a minute to wash myself."

"Go, boy," inspector Peter said, straightening one of the chaotically scattered chairs to sit down.

Maxim went to the toilet and the heaviness of confusion fell from his face right after the first contact with the water.

Countless thoughts flowed freely through his head. He stopped the water and agitated, he trembled. He felt a cold in his shoulders, so after wiping his face, he covered them for a moment, testing whether a dry cloth could help. His hands were clean. Inspector Dushan walked through the atelier, curiously looking at the various chisels, mixers, abrasives, blades and varnishes, lubricants, silicone tires, silicates, ceramics and other raw materials that were to be transformed into works of art. He stood in front of a metal stand where experimental clay mini models of male and female figures half-covered with old brown fabric were placed. He lifted the fabric and noticed a few colorful envelopes in the shape of regular hexagons.

Peter was sitting as if trying to look out the window.

"I think my hands are cleaner, gentlemen," Maxim said, still wiping himself, "do you want some coffee?"

"Not me," inspector Peter replied, turning to his colleague.

"I already had one, thank you," inspector Dushan added, stepping toward Maxim, "these envelopes smell... peculiar," he said, lifting them to his nose, which was absorbing them with varying intensity.

Clearing his gaze for a moment, Maxim grabbed himself by the throat and coughed.

"Yes... that's..."

"Don't have to tell me, you're not the only one with ... oh so exclusive passion for exchanging love letters at that age."

"Well, today the culture of sending letters is literally destroyed by the Internet, which is the reason why there are no epistolary novels. "

Dushan returned the letters, covering them again with the cloth.

"Tell me, young man, are you part of the rock band *Sagittarius*?"

"No, but I've had a few performances with them. Your colleagues have already asked me about that. Something about Jimmy again?"

"Probably not. As a matter of fact, we don't know who it is about."

"And..." Maxim hesitated, "what's the matter?"

"We don't know either," said the sitting inspector. "What we do know is that several people are missing. So far, we have recorded three, that is, four disappearances for which some of our colleagues suggest a connection."

Maximilian raised an eyebrow.

"Disappearances?"

The inspector got up and went to the table where there was a fruit dish.

"May I?" He asked, extending his hand to the dish, waiting for his interlocutor's confirmation.

The candy red strawberries were fairly small, but extremely juicy and sugary.

"Where do I throw this stem?" The inspector asked.

Maxim took an ashtray and left it on the table.

"They're missing, as far as we know," the inspector eye-shot him. "All of them women. Three of them are about your age, while the fourth is just over fifty."

"Hmmm... missing women. You made sure you didn't..."

"Sorry, I didn't finish," the inspector raised his voice almost imperceptibly, "what we also know, and what is particularly interesting about you and, of course, members of *Sagittarius*, is that you guys appear to be among the ones who were in the closest proximity to at least two of the ones missing when our sources last noticed them. As for you, young gentleman, we know you once made a statement at a station. Of course, the initial reason for your stay at the station was different from the one of our current curiosity", the inspector cleared his throat, "and it's really good that you've been, I guess, honest in the conversation with the chief inspector."

Maximilian sat down exhaling loudly through his nose,.

"Was the raid due to your suspicion that there was a kidnapper in the room?"

"The raid, boy, was due to a bunch of things. Including the suspicion that there was a kidnapper in the room or, God forbid, something worse."

Inspector Dushan, walking slowly around the room, carefully scanned every detail of the sculptures placed in the corners. He came to inspector Peter and, bending over, whispered something to him. Inspector Peter smiled and stood up, turning his gaze to Storge.

"I'm not an expert," he said, deepening for a moment, "but this statue seems almost divine and godlike."

Maxim nodded shyly.

"I really think so. And guess which part is my favorite. "

The sculptor raised his cheek in a half-smile.

"You guessed it, right?"

Inspector Dushan laughed, while inspector Peter shuffled with his right hand inside the coat, taking out a sheet of paper with four photos which he pointed at Maxim.

"I will ask only once: do you have any information about

the disappearance of the persons we are after?"

"Sir," Maxim muttered, "I can't discern what kind of connection could I or anyone from the band have with these girls..."

"Okay, your response from now on is recorded and our future actions will be based on it."

"But wait," Maxim turned to the photos, "I knew Alexandra and dr. Andrea..."

"Yes?"

"Of course I know Alexandra, she was the band's informal PR, while Andrea..."

5. Pragma

INTO THE SHOES OF SOBRIETY

Among the many fused scents in the atelier, one could still feel the one characteristic of the old worn-out police uniforms that Maxim recently recognized.

He sent the inspectors out and locked the door.

Sitting on the armchair, he took the envelopes.

The impatience screamed for them to open. Slowly. One by one.

The turquoise first. Beneath it were a dark yellow one, a sky blue one, and a purple one. A few plain white envelopes were placed at the bottom.

He read them fast and fully focused.

His goggled eyes were fixed on an abstract, motionless point below the imaginary horizontal margin that divided the field of view; the flicker was superfluous.

He shed a tear.

He got up and came to the wall, joining his lashes together.

The grinding of his clenched teeth produced a crackling sound reminiscent of some of the sounds of working with a chisel.

He squeezed his lashes tightly together and slammed his head against the brick wall.

The lacrimal glands, which at first trembled, now swayed in their full tilt.

In less than a minute, the rhythm of breathing accelerated to a haunting feeling of shortness of breath.

He slammed again. And again.

The crashing sounds of the banging were about to mimick a heartbeat until he made an unarticulated scream with all his strength, and a thin reddish jet cut his forehead in two, branching out, widening, extending to the temples, descending to the tips of the reddened cheeks.

A moment later, tears and blood crossed at the outer edge of his eyes.

Inside he felt an inevitable feeling of nausea. He had to go to the toilet.

Entering the toilet, he lifted the lid of the toilet bowl and began to vomit.

His face was hot.

When he was done, he took off his clothes and turned the water on.

He into the shower, grabbed the handle and aimed it at his chest.

Tears and blood blended with the water for a moment.

"Who am I, damn it?!"

***

"Dear Missionary of His Own Work,

every fear of yours is just a cursedly misunderstood and bloodthirsty dog, a mongrel which, the more you try to hit, the more stubbornly follows the path that leads to the ultimate truth of your actuality, and which you need to experience rather than understand.

You have to experience it until the end. You have to live it daily – your joy, your purpose, your spiritual food. Live your food, don't eat it bluntly. Taste your life. Live your style.

The fact that you are taking lives can seem daunting, but

that's exactly what your craft is! Your purpose! Theirs!

Daunting and sublime, and the real name of your sublimity is ascension. It is a process that lasts, sculptor!

For you it will last until the moment when, following my omens, you will reach the height where we will be able to communicate and express the truth about our supreme coalescence as equal beings. Call it according to your own choice: an angel-scribe, a poet of God, or Metatron.

You have been implicitly accusing me of the murders lately, in your pathetically subjectivized diary.

You are aware how fibbing and misleading from our truth it is, our impeccable unity of extraordinary opposites. You are not alone, you have never been. Just as you are physically born from another being, so your metaphysical essence originates from me.

The path to truth is ours. Ours. It is One and belongs to us. After all, the fact that the truth is always One is the reason why I do not tend to reappear in your dreams lately.

As you grow, so I ascend to the immeasurable heavens that belong to us.

Let us drink from the source of truth that belongs to us when we are thirsty and stay One with Passion.

Only two more sculptures separate you from the moment when you realize this yourself.

You are safe.

Overcome the shackles of fear with a breath of faith and fly.

Your darned half,
Charles."

Maximilian took out a sheet of paper and a pen.

He stopped shaking his hand, holding it with the other. Shortly afterwards, he managed to concentrate, began writing, and in a quarter of an hour it was over.

He put the paper in the envelope which he left next to

the others.

Leaving the atelier, he re-read the letter dozens of times.

He was carrying a heavy laptop case and several books.

The moment his feeling of a pulsation in his hand started to grow, he immediately sat on a bench in the middle of a nearby park to rest; everything was animated like never before. He just sat down, wanting to go back home.

Children played hopscotch.

He turned the page over, picked up a hard cover book to support it, and began writing. Shortly, he finished writing and left.

Opening the door, he left the sheet with the other envelopes on the table.

His eyes seemed to get out of control. It was as if he were aiming at a point beyond the surrounding materiality.

Bowing his head, he exhaled and left the room heading for the stables.

Artemio looked hungry. He got him some hay and a large, plastic red bucket of water.

***

After a long time, Artemio got a chance to take a walk away from the spacious yard of the atelier. He was now entering a forest where the old tall fir trees, the larches and the Macedonian pines mingled with the slightly younger and smaller, long ago bloomed black locust trees and fragrant acacias, quaking aspens, beech and maple trees, similar to the mingling of the countless birds' chirpings and the river murmurings.

The skin of the galloping animal shone like the several homogeneous clouds in the extraordinarily clean, bright sky, and the light accentuated the powerful muscles it used with a natural cause-and-effect minimalism, while playing with the numerous dust particles that, rising in the air, created figures in which complex mixtures of human, natural, and abstract shapes one could see.

Hours passed, and the sun signalled its imminent departure, as if pushed by the wind, which was slowly gaining its momentum.

After a long descent, having his eyelids languidly positioned halfway, the artist came across a bush fence and pulled the reins, deciding to spend the night there.

***

The evening in Marckest was hot and the birds that flew over the city after a successful hunt near the shore could be heard in the central town square.

Nearby, street performers were performing somersaults and acrobatics as advertisements for the night's circus show, accompanied by the penetrating smell of popcorn that street vendors were trying to sell at double the price to foreign tourists.

To the calmly moving Mariana, the whole atmosphere gathered countless childhood memories in one place, making her feel like a child again only for a second, without closing her eyes. She bought a small pack of popcorn from one of the sellers and had already eaten it halfway to Maxim's studio.

When she arrived, after repeatedly shouting his name, she realized the premises were empty. Gathering her lips in a circle, she hesitantly started to leave, but the very next moment she returned and put her palms on the doorknob. It was open. She got in.

It was freakishly incomparable to her last visit from more than a year ago.

"Gosh!" she exclaimed. "These are fine sculptures he did not bother mentioning..."

Carefully turning her head, she stepped through the space between the bravura creations, the chairs and the various tools.

She reached Eros and touched her forehead.

Staring at her for a moment, she turned her head toward

Ludus.

"Someone can come in and steal them... what a messy guy," she said, continuing to walk among the many scattered objects until she finally noticed a few clay figures on the metal stand. It looked as there was more under the fabric, so she picked it up, took one of the figures, looked at it closely, and sighed. It was dusty, she cleared it with her hands, and when putting it back down, she noticed several colorful, fragrant hexagonal paper pieces that looked like origami, and took the ochre-colored one.

Yes, those were such origamis that Mariana saw for the first time in her life. She took a closer look at them one by one. Although visibly bleached, the scents were still lingering.

***

The night spent under the open sky in the woods away from Marckest was neither new nor particularly breathtaking, although a necessary experience for Maxim.

Thousands of micro-dreams were scattered throughout his still-seedy consciousness, building together a colorful mosaic of memories, which in turn synthesized more or less ancient memories and visions of the future. He recalled in the dream that there was an unpleasant event with his childhood friends from the church, with an adult, an old man with long black mustache below the lip line, who talked about dealing with life's challenges and condemnation of the innate struggle for greater control over the world, then some red mini carousel with six seats. He also dreamed of scents, predominantly popcorn and cotton candy. There were others, but he forgot them a moment after he woke up. He knew that when he dreamed too much, there were only a few short, pleasant cuts left in the end, and the main message was forgotten.

***

The blonde, after settling for a minute looking at the envelopes, opened one.

"...But he was a prophet and knew that God had given him an oath that He would place one of his descendants on his throne. Foreseeing this, David spoke about the resurrection of the Christ, that He was not abandoned to Hades, nor that His body would see decay.[2]"

The mission had just begun.

With this, your ascension becomes an irreversible one-way process whose proper and complete execution is a matter of your superhuman, abstrusely technical readiness to create sublimity. You can feel how the fears are slowly leaving you in the world of the otherworldly things, where what was perceptible to the human senses also resides, a creature that falsely claimed to be the embodiment of Katya, with which you had to fornicate in that abominable shithole. As a ransom for this mortal sin of hers, be aware that, in the other world, the transformation into a tool for your Work will serve her, as it has just taken the first of The Six Forms.

Congratulations on the initiation.

Until our recent meeting,
H."

Mariana's fiery glowing eyes scanned the paper with a calm and immovable focus, and when she reached the last row, turned it to the other side. In the upper right corner there was a golden regular hexagon interspersed with three parallel red lines, the longest of which was the one in the middle, while the two on the sides were equal in length and formed two of the six hexagonal sides, reminiscent of Maxim's ruby ring.

She folded the sheet and blinked a few times.

Lost in thoughts, she closed her mouth with her index finger, focusing her eyes in the lower left corner for just over a minute, and then closed them.

***

Artemio rode across the coastline of the velocious, rugged and ever-changing Ryada river. The warm wind blowing in the faces of Artemio and Maxim carried a mixture of myriad scents: from linden and wild figs to lavender and rosemary, including the scents of countless more colorful meadow flowers. Carrying them, it seemed as if the wind had served Maxim his whole childhood right in front of his nose.

The incoming sun was still bearable, emphasizing through the reddish glow every inch of the muscular body of the massive horse..

Both chased hunger and thirst, but also all sorts of forgetfulness for physiological needs.

They wanted to travel more.

And yet, they were slowly arriving.

***

Among the variety of scents that could be felt in the room, it was extremely difficult to determine the dominant one. It was probably that of the sculptural varnish or the smell of clay that created the numerous miniatures arranged in an almost chaotic layout on the shelves, the floor, and the chairs.

Mariana returned the sheet in the hexagonal envelope and opened the next one.

"The girl preoccupying your mind is not a Muse, and you are very much aware of that. If she was, would she condition you with intermittently reinforcing demands and rewards? With such absurd barriers between your artistic but also human being and will? Both you and I know that the ultimate goal of your Work is to overcome physical limitations and ascend to infinity.

Well, in this pursuit she is an intruder, but also a helper; helper because of the mechanisms of motivation while we are in that world.

Your obsession with mortal pleasures, young man, fogs your vision, which is not only artistic. After all, art is your means of coming here.

You remember: while I was in that world, I once tried to show you that an artist always follows his own will, even under the threat of being beaten by everyday clowns who do not even know what will represents, let alone know it.

You have since learned that an artist without will is just a talented unit of the hoi polloi, but have forgotten that bums and intruders are here to test its strength.

Your will is altogether clear, firm and enticing like the ruby that adorns your extremely skillful fingers, and by being aware of it at all times, you are constantly working on your own exaltation and without any otherworldly figure or ostentatious girl reminding you of that.

Yes, that girl is my "helper", but her demands are personally hers, and not mine.

Her mission is to show you the way, and yours is to walk it.

Mine - with the last crumbs of your nature's mortality to sculpt the heavens to which you shall belong the moment you step here.

Be done with your crawling; everyone is waiting for your flight.

I send you the gentleness and warmth of the ubiquitous omnipeace here, already nestled in the ether through which you begin to acquaint vision.

TH"

Mariana took out one of the white envelopes and opened it.

***

The graceful movements of the white horse resembled flying; his tail was shaking in all directions, resembling the high-rising Sun with carelessly scattered rays, a baby rattle, or the experimentally playful brush from the student days.

The horse stopped near a shrub, when its rider descended but did not tie the animal. Artemio, confused, turned his head left and right, turned his eyes to the master, and let out a sound that sounded almost like a sigh. Maxim returned to him, stroked his lush mane, and unexpectedly poked him with a branch he broke from a nearby tree, and the horse slowly stepped forward.

Maxim tore off the small twigs from the branch and slashed vigorously, but the animal lovingly remained calm. He waved a few more times, as hard as he could, but the reaction remained the same.

The sculptor walked away, took few stones and threw them at the horse. After being hit by two, the animal stepped forward, emitting a penetrating, though not unbearably loud sound.

The artist continued walking.

The small pebbles of the narrow macadam easily penetrated in the thick sole of a semi-hard rubber and got stuck there. The path led upwards.

He walked up with a sense of ease.

Few fuzzy forests in the ardent greenery of the surrounding bushes distracted for a moment his otherwise immovably focused view, and after few minutes of minimal breathing, he allowed himself a moment for deep breathing.

Green summer widths stretched endlessly over the horizon, while the chirping of the nearby crickets was almost engulfed by the babbling Ryada, made playful by the wind.

There was a deepened semicircular segment of the riverbed that looked like a small bay in which the water was completely calm.

The reflection seemed to belong to someone else, from a well-known person whose name he could not remember. It was so crystal clear that he could recognize the turquoise color of the irises that penetrated through him.

The giant tree canopy of a nearby oak whose thick branches stretched over the river was in the background, as was the interior of the shore, almost touching with one side a huge rock.

The trunk was extraordinarily wide, and its bark had noticeable traces from cutting and unusual marks made of two horizontally placed hearts that touched the top in a single center. A dot was engraved above the center and a comma was under it, representing a semicolon symbol. Left and right there was a symbol that looked like a butterfly flapping its wings.

The cursed oak. The suicide tree. The wooden death.

Only few of the names of the century-old tree that had taken away so many young lives from Marckest by hanging.

The author of the symbol which appeared twenty or thirty years ago, was unknown, and rumors circulated that a father had come to cut the tree after the suicide of his daughter, but was attacked by a pack of wolves and forced to jump in the river and drowned.

Since then, no one had tried to disturb the natural tranquility of the cursed oak.

The author of the symbol was said to have been an artist, and the semicolon symbol was said to be an attempt to show the unfinished lives of those who came here with the intention of ending them.

***

"I must NOT, at any cost, give in to madness. To leave myself to a madman's wicked solutions. Do you read these letters? Yes? Why, curse you, whoever you are? Whoever I am,

I will not allow a destruction from within, and there are people in the world who will help me.

Cursed sadist!"

Mariana, breathlessly read the short letter word for word, and, making a few slow semicircles with her eyes, returned it in the plain, white envelope from which she had taken it.

***

Maxim was sitting on a thick solid oak branch above the river, his eyes dimmed by the shadow of the giant tree canopy. He could hear the rustling of unstoppable waves of accelerated water through the Ryada riverbed. The crickets and the chirping of many different birds from the surrounding area could also be heard.

It was not the first time he had sat on the branch. A month after coming to Marckest, after enrolling in the Faculty of Mathematics, realizing he had made the wrong choice, he was forced to move to the Faculty of Fine Arts, suffering from depression and a deep psychological crisis resulting from cultural shock and changing values. Until then, he had had his extremely idealistic vision of the struggle and aspirations in which life should be spent, full of artificially created, imposed challenges.

In his high school days, not being able to find proper companionship with his peers, he forgot himself into his own thought processed, thinking about his own thoughts, about God, subatomic particles, the universe, natural disasters, death, the structure of the cosmos, the Church, and pretty much most social phenomena. Searching for the ultimate truth for all final, satisfying answers, he began to create art by thinking in a systematic way.

Mathematics was his starting and final vision, his aspiration, his beginning and goal.

It was only after a few years that he was able to see and achieve some sort of balance in the extraordinarily complex intertwining of opposing mathematical theories of nature and art, for which he had inclination in his works.

The memories of the church, the childhood memories of his old neighborhood, the adventures with his earliest friends, and various short inserts of variety of colors, smells and sounds that, although had no content, brought his mind back to pleasantness.

Completely forgetting the time, he recalled traveling all over the Mediterranean, England, France, Scandinavia, then the quarrel with Jimmy after throwing a dirty sheet on the bed of their shared bedroom in Stockholm, the laughter of the whole class after persuading him to throw the music teacher's chair from the lecture hall on the third floor...

It seemed as if he had his eyes shut for hours, but he was able to keep them shut some more.

Nearby sounds resembling the movement of SUVs or big cars, could be heard, followed by some barking. He opened his eyes.

The water level was unusually high for this time of the year. He wondered how high was the natural pool under the waterfall at some fifty feet away, which one of the points where the view ended.

Closing his eyes again, he took the deepest breath possible and loosened his legs, which by then were tightly wrapped around the branch. The sounds of cars and of barking had now become quite clear and must have come from somewhere below.

He did not know if he should open his eyes again.

***

Mariana, stunned and with a look of astonished uncertainty, stared fixedly into the open letters. Biting her lips nervously, she returned to them again and again.

There were a few more unopened.

Touching her lips with her finger, she doubted if she wanted to continue before eventually taking one and getting up.

She took a glass from the table, went to the tap and filled it, then drank a few large sips before putting it back at its place, then began to look around, observing the statues, and finishing with the sculptural tools, placed in a wooden box not far from Storge, to which she approached and put her hands inside the sculpture.

There were all kinds of chisels, brushes, thin wooden

sticks that ended with rigid metal wires, saws and knives of various blades and sizes, from those with larger and smaller gears to butcher, thick and ordinary.

Swallowing thoughtfully, she turned her gaze to the door.

***

Maxim's eyes opened frenziedly, instantly pointing to the source of the sound.

He was right; they came from below, a small meadow far behind the waterfall where he wanted to end the whole thinking process, the torturous perceptions and the false reality they exposed. However, turning his head away, his thoughts took a different turn.

Down there were three barely visible SUVs. The police.

Several uniformed police officers parked outside. The barking was getting louder and louder.

After a few minutes, the dogs arrived. Four of them. They were on a leash and a differently uniformed officer tried to hold them. He raised his arm slightly and pointed down, while making some kind of circles with the other.

Two of the officers lit cigarettes almost simultaneously.

The other two got back in the SUVs and continued driving. The officer with the dogs, speaking on walkie-talkie, also went his way.

The barking dogs followed the water course.

Maxim's eyes, giving the impression of a peculiar, almost indifferent curiosity, tried to follow them before returning to the horizon.

"Hey, fool," a familiar female voice was heard from below.

He lowered his head. Just below, crossing the river, Katya was trying to hold on, looking more illuminated and clearer than the last time. Her hair was brown.

"Will you help me, silly?" She yelled. "If I fall, I will

drown."

"Go to hell," he said quietly.

"Did you say anything? I didn't hear you, louder!"

The artist lowered his eyelids in half.

"Maximilian!" Shouted Katya. "Please, come down here..."

"Why? You're aware you can't die."

"What? I don't remember saying I was joking. I don't remember any such moment. If I die... "

"Will love die in me, too?" He interrupted. "I already know what you're going to say."

"It's because..." She tried to hold on, "we're One."

The water level exceeded the height of her nose at times, so she raised her head spitting water.

Maxim closed his eyes.

"Maximilian!"

"Thank you for calling me by name," he replied, "but my love will not die the way you will. Death is a chaotic sand game mediated by the wind, and neither you nor my feelings are anything like sand. You are more like a tempest... "

At that moment the branch to which the girl was holding broke and she sailed downward.

"Help me! Help!"

Maximilian rolled his eyes and turned his head toward Katya. Accelerating his breathing, his face turned red for a moment.

He jumped.

The water there was colder than at any other point.

Katya was just a bit away, so he rushed towards her with a quick stroke. In panic, shouting his name, she waved her hands in an attempt to grab a tree trunk.

The tree was too far away, and the water was pulling both of them towards the waterfall.

***

"I, Maxim Comnenius, a renowned artist and a sculptor, appear to have a split personality with perfectly convincing hallucinations entering even the *normal* segment of my consciousness. I am, also, a murderer of women.

For me, this is the only objective reality, a tragic combination of circumstances in which day by day I lose hope for coping with it. After this self-acknowledgment, it is definitely too late for me to do anything..."

Mariana covered her eyes with her palm, inhaling as deeply as she could. Before proceeding with the reading, she took a few small sips of water. She lowered her glass while staring at an indefinite point between the statues; her eyelids merged spontaneously several times, with large breaks in between.

Turning her gaze to the letter, she continued reading.

"...Even if I managed to keep my mental problems under control by applying therapy, I could never forgive myself for these heinous crimes, and therefore, writing this confession, for me, this tragedy has just come to an end.

Fuck your immortality, your God's Throne, and your very existence.

I will decapitate the demon and will do that as soon as possible.

Greetings and until some more beautiful times and worlds,

Maxim Comnenius."

As they made big, abrupt moves, one by one, just before closing, Mariana's eyes dropped two barely noticeable teardrops.

***

The water flowing towards the waterfall was stunningly powerful and unstoppable, pulling the branches that Maximilian tore trying to grab one of the few river bushes the moment he reached Katya.

It all seemed completely lost until, a few feet below, and about forty feet from the waterfall itself, he came near the closest of the three large rocks in the midst of the river not far from the shore, where, with his arms wide, he managed to attach himself and hold on.

He inhaled and exhaled a lot of air through a few deep breaths and made a ladder with his hands allowing the girl to step onto his firmly joined palms and climb, and then he climbed at the top of the high rock himself.

"How did you get there, for God's sake?" He sighed.

Katya was slowly recovering.

"If you commit suicide, it would be a matter of time before my life is over."

Katya suddenly turned her eyes to his, holding her breath.

"What were you looking for in that tree?" He asked. "I guess you have a grasp of all that it symbolizes?"

Maximilian lowered his hands over Katya's thighs in a gentle hug.

"Let's go," he said, "c'mon, let's swim."

Katya closed her eyes, the sculptor faced the river and took her hand, lowering it to his belt.

"Hold as strong as you can and swim with me," he said, "the shore is within reach."

The girl nodded and they both went into the water at his signal.

Maximilian, dragged down by the water, managed to swim away with superhuman effort, enough to hold on to one of the bushes. Katya, who clung to him, managed to move to the other side of the bush, where even she could reach the soil with her feet. After coming to a solid standing point, he grabbed her by the arm and pulled her to shore.

The roaring waterfall was less than ten feet away.

Stepping on the shore, the artist let go of her hand.

Compensating for the consumed energy, he breathed

with his chests stretched out like the wings of some flying creature. After a while, he looked toward the waterfall.

There was no one.

***

Looking for water around one of the few undried springs of the natural canals that flowed into Ryada, Artemio pricked up his ears to the direction where the calls of his name were coming from by voice that sounded just like his master's. He raised his head above the chilly clear water in which he observed the reflections from the tops of nearby plants and turned back in the direction where he had come from.

Maximilian was approaching the place of separation with a quick step.

"Artemio! Artemio!" As he was screaming, the sinews in his neck stretched out.

He felt the closeness of the horse, just as he felt its arrival.

He saw him behind a bush at the end of a natural tree line that separated the river from the uneven path where they parted. Approaching him, he hugged him breathlessly.

Shortly afterwards, he found himself on its back again.

A melody with high choral tones from his childhood resounded throughout his mind, carrying a vague but pleasant atmosphere of transcendence and light whose resounding crescendo seemed to remind him of a long-heard, stern voice calling for attention. It seemed to him that he had heard it for the first time in a dream. It had been reappearing to him several times since then.

The trip to Marckest was a daunting task.

"Katya, bane of my hereafter," an unstoppable thought was perpetuating like a mantra, "whatever you aim at, you are about to sing the swan song aloud."

The horse galloped with full force towards the city, and not as late as his master predicted, he managed to reach it.

***

Before leaving the atelier, the musician opened the door and the windows. The air that filled the room ventilated the scent of a rose perfume, while allowing its pervading freshness to fill it up entirely.

Barely able to stand on her feet, she held her palm glued to her mouth. She filled another glass of water, drank it, and returned it to the table. After a while, she closed the windows and the door, and left.

***

The sculptor arrived at the gates breathless, sweaty and exhausted, but up until few minutes previously he gave the impression that he was no less vital than the Sun itself, whose light still refused to surrender to the night. However, the hours-long ride took its toll and he could hardly wait to surrender to her, to meet her in his dreams.

He left Artemio in the stables, changed his clothes, and entered the atelier.

"Appear, for God's sake," he whispered in the silence.

He closed his eyes as he walked forward, and then his nostrils trembled from the powerful inhalation, which ended in exhalation the very next moment when he opened his eyes. He looked at the door and one of the windows and come to it; in the distance, birds could be seen, changing their motions along with the rhythm of the songs, about to send the day away, and the grass was still shining.

He turned away with a downwards fixed look.

Stepping forward, he stopped for a moment in the middle of the space between the five sculptures and sat down.

"I can feel you, and you are forgetting that," he whispered.

The one who was called upon appeared from behind the wall on his right. Maximilian turned his gaze to the table and to the glass on it.

"I can't forget," the girl said with a smile, "I'm not

enough... mortal to forget forgetful artist."

She engraved her gaze at the glass, through which transparent glow a web of rays' reflections coming from different angles could be seen, colored in countless colors. But it was as if there was something else around her. After a short while, slowly lowering his eyelids, he moved his irises slowly to the left. And then it felt as if they had descended by themselves.

"You seem to have forgotten again: The work is waiting for you," she whispered, "and me along with it. And if you have another choice..."

"I haven't forgotten," he tried to answer, losing the battle against sleep.

***

On the edges of the dark floating silhouette around the Heretic's head seen from behind, it was as if a spider's web was woven, or perhaps a maze of different light shades, brighter than any crown or halo. A maze that looked familiar.

As he walked away, it looked even more so. It had a hexagonal, diamond-like shape, open for entrance only from below.

"Come in, restless man," the silhouette murmured.

Unknown forces suddenly seized his body, moving it towards the speaker.

He struggled to get rid of them with every cell of his body, but success was not achieved

"The diamond you are afraid to catch will take your wealth away."

The force was pulling harder. The act of giving in to her seemed both as the artist's own will, but also, to a certain extent, to someone else's. He could not determine why any, and all further questions, faded on their own.

"You're a diamond, a sculptor."

"You really think that?"

"I do."

"You suppose I'm just a bee destined to enter the cells of

your honeycomb?"

"Young man, I don't need your juices."

"You need my labor."

"Your labor is a discipline of sublimity and you know best who needs it."

He could not determine whether he had gradually lost his strength or depleted his will to defend himself.

Entering from the lower side of the maze, he reconcilingly closed his eyes, and suddenly, the whole maze turned upside down. The walls were redistributed, directing the entrance i.e. the exit upwards.

***

"Hey," Jimmy said calmly.

Maximilian gawked, then closed his eyes again in a second.

The rocker exhaled. White line remnants of dried tears could be seen on the edges of his face, while fresh new ones descended on the middle of the cheeks.

"I need you," he said.

"What happened?" Maxim asked half-heartedly.

"My dad."

"What's wrong with him?"

"He's in custody. Or... he was" Jimmy replied, covering his eyes with his hands.

"Did something happen?"

"He's got 4 stabbing wounds from a sharp window bar. A prisoner who was in the same cell with him before they moved him, was a religious zealot... he learned about what he had done... and intercepted him in the detention unit before the dinner break."

"Oh Lord!"

"He's been in the ICU since last night."

"Want me to come with you?"

Gathering his lips inward, Jimmy nodded in agreement.

***

Evening.

Outside, lively folk melodies of wedding trumpets accompanied by a penetrating male baritone and rarely high female soprano, sliced the air.

The thunderous buzzing of the car engines at the moment when they passed the Mariana's room, who was clutching her legs on the bed, could also be heard.

Someone knocked on the door.

"Your cell phone is ringing," a man's voice was heard from the other side. "Did you hear me?"

"Let it ring," the girl replied.

"Okay, I'll leave it by the mirror."

The voice left.

Mariana's eyes were preoccupied with following a fixed point in the middle of the colorful covers of a childhood photo album.

The very next moment she decided to get up. Unlocking the door, she came to the mirror, and lifted the phone with her head down. Slowly moving her left hand over her scalp, she dialed three numbers with her right.

"Good evening, Marckest Police Department. How can we help you?" A woman's voice was heard.

The musician's trembling lips made a double arc similar to one during a typical smile, and in just few moments, separated only millimeters from two tears coming from her right and one coming from her left eye.

"Hello? Is everything alright?"

She turned off the phone while kneeling down, bursting into loud cries.

***

The flood of people through the city's main hospital complex was one of the most colorful in Marckest; Thousands of young and old, men and women, running or hardly mobile due to disability or momentary inability to move, rushed to various destinations, entangled in a chaotic network of accelerated passengers intercepted on all sides by noisy and unstoppable car traffic.

The surgery clinic was located in one of the most spacious buildings in the very center of the complex.

That Tuesday afternoon, the Intensive Care Unit was entirely hushed, but for the rock guitar riffs followed by bits of singing on the radio from the nurses station that reached room 213.

The doctor entered, while talking to one of the nurses and asking her to bring food.

As she walked through the space between the four bedrooms, while the doctor was giving suggestions for each patient's food, Jimmy, with his face down and his fingers crossed, tried to interrupt, but in vain. Finally, the doctor came.

"Are you the son?" He asked, waiting for Jimmy's affirmative nod. "I will not sugarcoat this, I will be direct. Your father is in critical condition. Do you understand?"

Jimmy's eyes seemed to rise on their own. His hands parted: he lowered his left, and with the index finger of his right he supported his jaw.

"The attack was carried out sideways, from behind and from the left. Two of the stab wounds are lateral, the other two – posterior. One of the laterals hit the left suprarenal vein. This almost completely avoids a direct kidney puncture. On the other hand, the patient has lost a substantial amount of blood, which, as you are informed, resulted in a pre-comatose state. The organs were not injured, but two of the stab wounds affected the venous plexuses and the posterior spinal arteries, mostly in the lumbosacral region. I would like to inform you that such bleeding is, broadly speaking, dangerous on its own, and can lead to spinal cord damage, and thus possible motor disorders, loss of muscle control and a number of other disorders. Fortunately, we are almost convinced that this is not the case with your father. "

"How much blood did he lose, Doctor?"

"Enough to bring him in a pre-comatose..."

"Will he survive?"

"We've had worse cases. We are monitoring the situation closely," the doctor said, looking at the clock on the wall.

"All right, but tell me, what would the consequences be?"

"We know as much as you do. The bleeding has stopped, but his condition is far from stable. Let us give him some time."

"What do you mean? Is it... "

"Young sir, I'm leaving now. Another intervention awaits me. I will explain the details as soon as we have anything new. And please do not stay here long. I deliberately broke the rules by letting you enter because, despite everything, as a human being, not as a doctor, I do believe you should be able to see your father. "

"Sure, doc. Thank you."

Nodding, the doctor stepped toward the door.

Maxim came to Jimmy, leaning his arm on Jimmy's shoulder with half his weight.

"He's my father," Jimmy whispered through his mouth. His eyelids were half closed.

Charles entered the room through the wall on the top right corner.

"It will be fine," he murmured with a cynical smirk.

The weeping Jimmy couldn't notice him with his head turned down. Maximilian's lips twitched nervously, followed by a sudden outburst of rage reddening his face, goggling his eyes warningly.

In the room no. 213 of the ICU, the Heretic's winged silhouette hovered over the beds with the patients' immobile bodies.

His immovably pointed cheeks appeared as solitary mountaintops in the middle of an expressionless poker face, but Maximilian could already feel it was just a mask. Barely refraining himself to run in an attempt to punch him with several full-blown strokes of the fists, he managed to control the urge, exhaling his anger, closing his eyes, and then turning to his friend.

"Your cell phone is ringing," he told him, noticing the vibration in his pocket.

Jimmy took out his phone.

"Yeah?"

"Jimmy..." Mariana's voice was heard, "I have something important to talk to you about. Where are you?"

"In hospital."

"Are you alone?"

"No, with Maxim."

"Oh, okay. Talk to you later. "

"Until then," Jimmy replied, returning the cell phone in his pocket.

CREATION NO. 5

"The death of the profane and superfluous things is the cornerstone of creation of the sublime," the artist said to himself, walking carefully through the blind cobblestone alley. Late in the night which was strewn with rare, tiny cold drops that stuck to the face like sweat, the urge to create by removing harmful excesses was the strongest.

Passing through the narrow alleys, he never turned his head.

His footsteps were as strong as the unwonted hammer on the belt under his black coat that deftly played with the light dew - blunt mind as if stuck in its own loneliness , on the one side; a surgically piercing blade on the other.

Were it not for the dim light coming from the dilapidated pole fifty feet away, it would have been pitch black. Not even a single beam of light could be seen through the windows of the surrounding houses.

Twenty steps from the pole was the entrance to the city cemetery. Passing the threshold, he lowered his hood. In a few minutes the dew had completely disappeared. Just a bit more; the goal was just within the sight. He rested his elbow on a cross-shaped tombstone. And there he was. The wind blew tomb flowers scents all over, and the artist could distinguish each of them.

The marble flanneur was soon to be dust made of marble

memories. The poor man whose metaphors did not leave the mind indifferent even after his demise.

Immobile and white. Static imitation of one's own death.

Exact embodiment of the transcendental evil, immanently omnipresent in all the worlds it would enter. It was too late to prevent the terribly painful end enchanted by the scents of flowers. The heretic had to die.

Maximilian ran out, taking his hammer and turning it with his blade forward, towards the large white statue. He swayed full-bloodedly and with all his might, hitting and breaking its legs first. The statue collapsed, and Maximilian continued to strike the neck, the shoulders, the arms, and the torso.

The scent of lavender, partially muffled by that of incense and lilac, penetrated the nostrils, flowing through the chest, bringing joy to the moment of absolute freedom and harmony that lead a flawless creation to become part of a distinct, above-earthly world. After all, the smells themselves seemed to already know him. Maybe they were showing the way forward. That poetry of the here and the present, even if only a sensory presence, reminded of the church, but much more - reminded of the long-established memory, the earthly empyrean of childhood. The amplitude of Maximilian's breathing did not give the impression that it would be the main reason to stop; he hit with all his furious tenacity, everywhere.

After knocking it down with just one lightning blow, he spared only the head. With the sharp part of the hammer he tore it off and set it aside, allowing himself a moment's respite, so in the next one he could get back to the rest of the sculpture, which began to look more and more like white marble dust ready to dissolve in a dew-water puddle. It resembled white magic preparing to conquer black magic, imposing over the sorcerer–victim.

The shattered statue could not experience the rage of the outcast from its tormentful spirit, the one who seemed kindred in soul, artistry and knowledge, but in comparison to whom he considered himself wiser. The shattered statue could not know what pain was, because it was a statue, a shattered one. The scents, accompanied by memories of carefree freedom, penetrated the soft air, and Maximilian's body swirled around the imaginary axis, spinning with the help of a massive tool made of shiny steel, blunt on one side and sharp on the other.

This division allowed him to choose between giving strong, blunt, crushing blows, and those that cut, tore, and refined as needed. Something like the ordinary, despicably common man who, if he was to achieve a higher, material life purpose, he succeeded aptly and in harmony that seemed surreal, to combine the sharp and blunt aspects of his personality.

***

In the third room to the east, the boiling sounds of hot liquid bronze could be heard in the heated metal cauldron, ready to pour Pragma's body, which lacked only a head. The sculptor carefully discharged the liquid into the ceramic mold when he heard the discreet ringing of his cell phone. Twenty minutes after over the ringing stopped, he picked up the phone and dialed the number from the missed call.

"Hello?"

"Hey," Jimmy's voice was heard, "I thought about everything and... I'm going to Sweden. I received an offer to work at an elite hotel."

"Are you serious?"

"Yes," he said in a distant voice, "and, yeah, my father died."

Maxim took a glass of whiskey and, pouring the barley bourbon, knelt down, taking a sip.

"They just called me."

"May God rest his soul."

"Gotta take this chance, Max. For me and my son. In the long run, there is no bread for artists in this shithole. Soon there will be no water, also. There will be only wine left for the sinners. Anyway… the funeral is tomorrow at noon."

"Alright."

"Adieu, Max."

The bronze was hardened, and the decapitated statue was prepared for the sand-clearing gush from the sandblaster. The sculptor turned it on. This time, the night did not cause a dream. The sculptor worked tirelessly and energetically on his new construction, building the perfect imaginary whole of all the segments. For a moment, his hand trembled unusually, forcing him to repeat the movements several times, but that did not refrain him from what he had in stall.

The statue welcomed the new day with a head; coarsely realistic, majestic, almost unearthly, yet remarkably natural female head merged with the rest of the body with a thick layer of metal, posting a lavish and lush glow in the embrace of the morning Sun; a glow that almost deprived her of the need for patina and additional ornaments beside the olive branch in her hair.

The head looked up at the light coming out of the window, a few inches above the fingers of its left hand.

6. Agape

THE LEAVING

The front and rear entrances of the cemetery were under the watchful eye of the police. Parts of them were barricaded and closed to newcomers who had to follow a strict moving protocol in order to reach the graves.

A sexton and a gravedigger answered questions from the police inspectors, who recorded the statements in notebooks.

The closing of part of the cemetery and the strong police surveillance were the reasons why the funeral of Jimmy's father was delayed by almost an hour. The procession grew in numbers and reached around a hundred, led by the priest reciting New Testament passages aloud not with his loudest voice:

"Then I saw another mighty angel coming down from heaven. He was robed in a cloud, with a rainbow above his head; his face was like the sun, and his legs were like fiery pillars. 2 He was holding a little scroll, which lay open in his hand. He planted his right foot on the sea and his left foot on the land, 3 and he gave a loud shout like the roar of a lion. When he shouted, the voices of the seven thunders spoke.[3]"

Sylvester and Maxim, side by side, struggled to grasp the priest's words at the tail of the crowd.

"Murder," Sylvester whispered, looking at the police.

Maximilian turned his gaze in the same direction.

"How do you know?"

"A pal in the police told me. Brutal beating. Some freaking maniac cut off the victim's head."

The sculptor startled.

One of the elders in the procession turned, interrupting the drummer's murmuring with a warning look.

The priest moved the candle back and forth in semicircular hand gestures, continuing his speech: "After this I looked, and there before me was a door standing open in heaven. And the voice I had first heard speaking to me like a trumpet said, 'Come up here, and I will show you what must take place after this.' At once I was in the Spirit, and there before me was a throne in heaven with someone sitting on it. And the one who sat there had the appearance of jasper and ruby. A rainbow that shone like an emerald encircled the throne. Surrounding the throne were twenty-four other thrones and seated on them were twenty-four elders. They were dressed in white and had crowns of gold on their heads. From the throne came flashes of lightning, rumblings and peals of thunder. In front of the throne, seven lamps were blazing. These are the seven spirits of God. Also, in front of the throne there was what looked like a sea of glass, clear as crystal. In the center, around the throne, were four living creatures, and they were covered with eyes, front and back. The first living creature was like a lion, the second was like an ox, the third had a face like a man, the fourth was like a flying eagle. Each of the four living creatures had six wings and was covered with eyes all around, even under its wings. Day and night, they never stop saying:

'Holy, holy, holy is the Lord God Almighty,'
who was, and is, and is to come.

Whenever the living creatures give glory, honor and thanks to him who sits on the throne and who lives for ever and ever, the twenty-four elders fall down before him who sits on the throne and worship him who lives for ever and ever. They lay their crowns before the throne and say:

'You are worthy, our Lord and God to receive
glory and honor and power.
For you created all things, and by your will

they were created and have their being.'[4]

The priest turned to Jimmy, spraying some liquid under his feet.

Then, rotating, he made a semicircle in both directions facing the crowd and crossing himself three times, calmly said: *Amen.*

Shortly afterwards, the coffin was lowered into the ground.

SPLIT

Jimmy, Sylvester, Philip and Simon, while entering the premises of the nation-wide "Portal FM" radio station located on the ground floor of the only white-yellow complex in between the reconstructed red buildings, came across the host, Mark. He read the news in a micro room separated by a window and greeted them with a "sit-down smile", signaling them to get to their places.

"...The upcoming parliamentary elections, as has long been speculated in the public, are likely to take place next year, senior government sources told the State Information Agency. In a statement to Portal FM, the coordinator of the parliamentary group of the largest ruling party, Xamil Mensuik, said the election was likely to take place in fall, not ruling out the possibility of holding simultaneous parliamentary and presidential elections. Mensuik also expressed the ruling party's readiness to run in the upcoming elections, stressing their conviction in a decisive, sixth election victory in a row...

The Ministry of Interior Affairs said that there had been significant progress in the investigation into the female bodies found buried on the shore of Ryada River. The Ministry confirmed that the individuals were recorded under the *Kidnappings & Missing Persons* graph, and there were already speculations in the media about their connection. The claim of the investigative journalist Leon Bethlem from the magazine

"Insider" that this is a serial killer who systematically removed organs, i.e. parts of the bodies of his victims, as of now has not been officially confirmed or denied. According to Bethlem, the body parts that were removed are: a female sexual organ along with the womb, the legs, the arms and the chest. A ministry spokesman asked the media to refrain from public dissemination of information Bethlem's information, saying all details regarding the investigation would be made available in, as he put it, a manner that would not jeopardize its progress and thus prevent any further escalation.

And another case on the topic – a decapitated body of a 46-year-old woman was found in the Marckest City Cemetery. The forensics team working on the case confirmed that the victim was brutally beaten and dismembered by the usage of a cold weapon, which allegedly removed her head. Some of the staff of the City Cemetery have speculated about the victim's identity, stating the possibility that the woman was a regular visitor to her son's grave after his recent death... And finally, something less macabre, related to sports..."

Jimmy and Sylvester, raising their eyes, unconsciously met them at an imaginary point in the middle of the ceiling.

Shortly afterwards, Mark finished with the announcements and approached them.

"How are you guys doing?"

"Hanging in there," Sylvester replied shortly.

"It's always important that you hang in by yourselves."

"If we were hung by others, we'd be more likely to end up at the gallows."

Mark, always grinning, offered them a drink. Jimmy refused.

"Ready?"

Sylvester and Philip nodded.

"Alright, wait a minute for the commercials to end and we'll start."

The interview, which consisted of standard questions about some of the meaningful past experiences, plans to expand professional collaboration, possible tours, new singles and albums, lasted about twenty minutes. Then the host, constantly trying to involve all four of them equally in the conversation, gave them space to perform two of the brand-new songs, and after that calls from listeners were expected.

****

"Hello," a woman's voice was heard on the other side of the line, "I'm calling from an office two blocks away. I am a former... friend of the band *Sagittarius*, especially Jimmy, whom I'd like to greet and wish him to find himself a serious female partner to celebrate his birthday with as soon as possible, which, by the way, is on December 1, one of the two days in the year when you can get free condoms."

"Nice touch," Mark laughed.

"And if that fails, you can try with a male partner any time. Don't need to cover it up, nor you need to talk yourself out of your homo or bisexuality by redeeming into the life of an utterly decadent male whore, Jim. You've run out of gas, pal, and everyone can see that. No matter how much your father tried to convince you in the opposite..."

"Sylvia, you, twat. You hit the right timing, pouring your low passions out by publicly insulting my dead father," Jimmy said, "but know one thing: if I were gay, I would have socialized, not fornicated with you, my dear."

"You're not active, Jim. Probably just a passive homo. Still, you should let people know. I mean, after letting yourself know first and stop raping yourself... "

"Alrighty... Mark... " Jimmy gestured Mark to stop the conversation.

"Okay, that's it. Please free the line for the next listener who will not use vulgarities and will respect the elementary code of ethics for public behavior. We continue with such caller, I hope, since I'm told we have someone else on the line."

"Good day," said a familiar female voice.

"Mariana..." whispered Sylvester.

"I call to welcome the constant efforts you are making on the music scene to revive and bring the least popular rock subgenres closer to the audience, which already is able to recognize you and I have no doubt it will continue to distinguish you among all the others."

"To distinguish *us*," said Philip.

"Let them recognize *you*, Phil. I'm done with music."

The four of them met eyes with each other.

"Don't get me wrong, my experience with you guys has been marvelous and I would never regret a bit about our work, but as you know... inexplicable things happened, or at least things that seemed so until recently, and which, at least for the time being, seem a lot clearer to me."

"What things, Mariana?" Philip asked.

"Things that have led to the Oneness of creative minds turning into ouroboros, a snake eating its own tail. Even if they happened unknowingly."

"I do not understand you. But I don't think we're at the right place to discuss our internal stuff. "

"There are external subjects, Phil," said Mariana, "who are in one way or another absorbed by the band, or the band is absorbed by them, and who really could not be isolated from the course of action that led to its curse, swallowing human destinies like Atropa cutting off the living threads of mortals.

And I don't regard myself a divine creature or a curse."

"Mariana, I can't listen to you talking like this," Simon said as he approached the microphone, "please, listen to me."

The fixed looks of everyone gave the impression of extreme fervor mixed with a migratory impulse of prickling agitation.

"No, Simon," Mariana interrupted, "you and your bass guitar are everywhere anyway. You'll have to listen to me this time. I want to remind you... you are aware that the Demiurge did not create all of us from the same divine dust. For some it shines with blinding force, for others just enough to light the way for them and maybe a few more, and for some it is like a star melted into endless darkness. You know that neither you nor I belong to the first and the third."

Philip looked up in utter confusion.

"But you also know that there are those who belong to both." Please, try to understand."

"Mariana, you..."

Sobbing, the girl interrupted him once more.

"No matter how far I'm going to be from here in a few hours, I will remember you forever for the profound and exquisite, yet now buried beauties, that I lived with each one of you. Even with those who bury others."

"Oh my God..." Philip exclaimed in a seemingly more indifferent tone.

"Bye, buddies," said the girl before cutting the line.

"Dear listeners," said Mark, "after the ad break, we return to the studio. Stay tuned to Portal FM."

CREATION NO. 6

The raw materials in one half of the main room of the studio were chaotically scattered, and yet, the space around and between the sculptures was emptied and now even completely cleared of various trifles that gave the impression of a messy piece of space.

In the middle there was a properly placed hexagonal bronze plate, from which a low circle-shaped pedestal was raised. The transition of the hexagon to a circular shape was gradual, slowly melting the angular sides into completely oval shapes.

At the farthest end, in a straight line at the entrance, a newly welded bronze statue of Agape descended, embodied in a radiant girl whose left hand was between her chest and neck, and her right, with her palm and index finger pointing up at the sky. Her face was ennobled with an innocent smile, revealing her teeth behind her wide smiling lips, which were about to start trembling any moment in a blissful grimace.

Her eyes were wide and deep, her nose straight, her neck elegantly slender, ending in a lanky and delicate clavicle under which her breasts gradually emerged, one of which was exposed.

In the middle between the breasts, it was as if a thin line was beginning to look like a gash; it curved under the left breast, ending on the left side near the thin ribs.

The torso and the legs radiated with the same trembling liveliness as every other part; unlike all the previous statues, in Agape there was not a single segment that was more accentuated than the others, when shape was concerned.

Her proportions seemed to have been calculated for years, and her very creation seemed to be the result of a surgically precise, detailed operation that in no way resembled the previous works of the sculptor.

***

There was a strong, yet not cold wind that sent away the day which at times was even humid, while Mariana was weeping and turned off her cell phone and put it in her pocket.

Taking a handkerchief, she wiped away her tears and hurried across the boulevard, reaching a rather neglected open-air amusement park and continued towards one of the fanciest restaurants.

She was rushing by the empty swings with her thoughts frost, slightly holding her head with her right hand. She had to go to the bathroom urgently, not knowing if she would be able to hold it until she reached the restaurant. A colossal tunnel-like structure appeared in front of her - the inactive and abandoned rollercoaster was the home of the many colorful bumper cars fostered by the old operator who was faithfully dedicated to his newspaper and his radio. She decided to take a left turn from there toward the toilet, continuing her way on the asphalt road.

Few steps from -a small wooden shack next to which a gray van was parked, it seemed to her that she had heard footsteps. However, as she turned around, she did not notice anyone. The only sounds that could be heard were coming from the old radio.

Mariana scratched her shoulder and forcibly opened the massive wooden door with cracked paint and continued to the women's toilet. Entering, she locked the door and opened the bag, taking out a box of some medicine and two pills. She drank them promptly.

The moment she sat on the toilet, the front door opened.

The steps were not at all quiet.

Cold shivers ravaged every inch of her body.

Instinctively stopping her breathing, she got up and turned to the window.

It was too small even for a purse to pass through.

The crackling of the wooden floor under the dusty carpet in the hallway that separated the men's and the women's toilets echoed louder and louder, making her muscles tremble uncontrollably.

Her cell phone was in her purse.

She put her hand in quietly. She knew exactly where it was, managing to touch it with her fingertips.

In an instant, a deafeningly thundering strike sent all her weight in her heels.

Screaming as loudly as possible, she headed for the shabby public shower room trying to find a hard object.

The figure on the other side of the door slammed again, several times in a row.

The fight-or-flight-fallen blonde, shouting, entered the shower cabin and grabbed the metal shower handle, trying to unhook it but it was in vain.

The door was half-closed, and the stranger kept hitting it and the lock was about to fall off.

Seeing that she could not remove the massive metal element, the blonde reached for the vertical metal frame from the shower cabin. With a few strokes she managed to detach it from the longitudinal structure, holding it firmly with both hands.

"Maximilian! Maxim! "Shouted the girl, "I know it's you!"

The lock loosened completely, and the broken door opened slightly.

"Maximilian! I know you're unaware of all this!"

Then, the door opened entirely.

"That monster is not part of you! I know you better than all the rest!" She shouted through tears.

The figure, dressed in a black coat, stepped forward.

Maxim entered.

He held the hammer in one hand and a towel in the other.

"You know it's me... you know me... am I hiding?" He asked, staring up and down Mariana's legs and eyes.

Mariana, breathless, squeezed the metal frame tightly.

"Maximilian, you're not what..."

"Yes, I'm not..." the artist closed his eyes for a moment, and immediately afterwards opened them with a sigh, directing them downward.

"I'm not what those who aren't me say," he murmured, closing his eyes and stepped towards the blonde.

She made a piercing shriek while swinging the metal object from the left side upwards.

The artist, staring at her, rejected the blow with a simple defensive move, making a semicircle with his right hand and at the same time moving his body forward, managing to put himself in front of her.

Throwing the hammer aside, he grabbed her hand and, rotating his own body so that he be behind the girl, forced her to lower the metal rod. The next moment, he put the towel around her mouth and her nose.

The girl waved her arms and her legs, trying to hit him, but in a very short time she lost her strength and began to feel like she was sinking into a pleasant sleep.

The towel smelled of something pleasantly moist. Sugary, fruity sweet, and sour alcoholic moisture in which one could feel the remnants of scents of a hospital.

For a whole minute she tried to hit Maxim, but each subsequent move became weaker and more inaccurate, as did her voice, which became quieter from moment to moment.

"Forgive me, M... for nothing in this world is personal..." he lifted her on his shoulders, came out of the shower cabin and lowered her in front of the van for a moment.

He took the keys out of his pocket, unlocked the trunk, picked up the girl and put her inside.

"Nor eternal," he said, closing the trunk.

***

The Special Operations Task Force joint office at the Marckest Police Department was surprisingly crowded with inspectors and other police officers staring at the monitors, moving, analyzing and showing one another various documents, running in all directions.

Inspector Peter entered and went to the desk of the young inspector with a properly trimmed mustache.

"Even if she didn't refer to him, we do have grounds for a search," he said.

"I had grounds to change his facial proportions even when we booked him," the young inspector replied, "I should have crushed the bastard."

"Prepare that part of the recording, I wanna listen to it again," said inspector Peter.

The young inspector turned on a recording of Mariana's phone on the frequency of "Portal FM" with a few clicks on the screen of the black PC. After the approval of inspector Peter, he played it.

"...There are external subjects, Phil, who are in one way or another absorbed by the band, or the band is absorbed by them..."

"Pause," said inspector Peter.

The young inspector cast a questioning glance at his superior. After a brief thinking, inspector Peter announced:

"All right, go on."

The young inspector continued playing the tape.

"... and who really could not be isolated from the course of action that led to its curse, swallowing human destinies, like Atropa cutting off the living threads of mortals."

Inspector Peter turned his head away.

"All right, you can turn it off."

Slowly, deliberately raising his walkie-talkie, he stuck his glance at the neo-expressionist painting of a house with a child in front of it and a light blue background, hanging on the wall in front of him.

"I think we are ready for action," he said.

***

Katya's body was trembling with excitement that she would be able to reach the Light to which she belonged. She was blindfolded due to the habit of mortals to look at things selectively and also, to finally stop being afraid of the Ascension.

Her hair this time was white as the Light which omnipresence could already be felt.

The godly Agape was almost ready, as was the substance.

Maximilian went to the stove and lifted the bowl of heated bronze, then brought it to the statue.

The letters were now meaningless, so one by one, he threw them into the liquid metal, finding their meaning in unity with the substance which divine transformation was to take place soon, terribly soon.

In front of the immeasurably merciful feet of Agape, who prayed with all her being, surrendering herself completely to heaven, laid the body of the bound, trembling and blind as usual Katya, waiting for the Unity with the eternal, omnipresent Spirit.

But before that, she was to experience the one who was striving to become one himself, and the moments of that process were limited, although useful in themselves.

One by one, the moments became like tiny, dense drops of autumn rain that simultaneously caressed and cleaned the streets and the misty Marckest air. Rain, after its ending, inspired by the yellowing of the leaves, one could feel the nourishing viridity of the greenery and the chlorophyll.

One by one, the touches became more and more present.

One by one, each penetration in the womb of the perfect woman seemed to be an act of blessed creation in itself, a sigh of the Cosmos which, thinking of itself, understood its own purpose.

Katya, more visible, brighter than ever, really became part of Maximilian's world, a realm to which she truly belonged.

Combining the essence of bodies and beings in the act of perfect Love, the sculptor praised the Muse for keeping her promise.

The woman, the statue and the angel merged in Trinity represented a perfectly shiny metal, a mirror spilled into another, a mirror of a mirror of a mirror.

Maximilian, The Heretic, and Katya were the serotonin, the adrenaline, and the oxytocin of the Universe, its Father, its Son, and Holy Spirit, its light, its material manifestation, and its shadow hanging like an island around, but only as an integral segment of it.

The artist used the hammer blade to open the statue in the area through the chest where the line passed. Maximilian opened Katya's chest, feeling every flicker in the game of the heart, which called, shouted, to be taken and used for its heavenly purpose.

Even the special force units of the Police Department, immeasurably far from the truth about the blood that seemed as spilled, entering the atelier, at least for a moment looked as if they had noticed it.

Neither with their semi-automatic rifles nor with shouting did they stop the Ascension.

Returning the heart back to the statue, he poured the metal liquid and closed the chest of the ultimate statue. Cosmic ordination had begun and the portal to immortality, the route to athanasia had been opened. Holding the hammer down, Maximilian stepped toward the middle of the hexagon, his altar.

He finally stopped, being absorbed as he absorbed it into him himself.

His breathing, just like the darkness around, was losing

momentum, each subsequent breath becoming shorter.

His legs were slowly, happily detached from the stairs made of the noblest material from which he himself had been built until recently. Walking upstairs, he was becoming calm that the pinnacle was within reach. The calm dance of the lashes slowly became superfluous, merging them into an embrace.

He raised his hammer, and the special units that surrounded the area shouted some warning words, and one of them, just a moment later, fired a shot.

In vain. The deity was touched, but not by the bullets coming from behind.

Still unconvinced, one of the uniformed men fired again, this time from the front. He did not feel the need to keep his eyes open when the absolute world of noumena witnessed him in the way he had aspired since the days spent in the cathedral, turning it into an everyday dream. The pinnacle was here.

The uniformed men ran around the altar, not threatening its sanctity even the slightest.

On the contrary, as they approached it, their bodies became blurred and dimmed. At one point, trying to enter his sacred space, they disappeared.The liberating smile on Maximilian's face was another portal to eternal euphoria and beatitude.

He finally acquired the wings that took him higher than any sky in existence, and there was no need to turn his head down.

For a moment, conquering the heights of the highest and brightest of the most luminous among the angels, he apprehended that writing the letters as unavoidable apparatus of pious joy and clemency was a process that, like his flying upward, had to be carried on.

BETWEEN FICTION AND REALITY

(Stemarcus, Letters Of Heresy)

Here is, at last, a sophisticated novel that fully meets the criteria of our modernity, namely the requirements of the modern readership, thirsty for works that will unravel some of the secrets of the inter-space between spirit and body, between tenderness and roughness, and of the space between reality and fiction, desire and achievement on one hand, and the sublime paradigm of the aesthetic of the primeval literary writings engraved in ancient myths and old recorded writings, through all literary formations that metaphorically, and even more literally "flirted" with them, with the myth and the testament, to the attested truths through the filters of modern art, in which the recognizable leads to self-unrecognition, and even more so that it corresponds to modern paradigms in science, set in theories whose main goal is not only to respond strictly to their fixed realms, but even more to "coquettishly and fantastically flirt" with virtual the elusive paradoxes of man, nature, and society, from the ancient mysteries immersed in names (nomination theory) and numbers (set theory), to semiotics (in which each sign has its place in the system) and cybernetics, which increasingly confronts us with the delusion of personal superiority in space and time, in the recurrence of self-perfection precisely through the modeling of reality according to the self and the other not so much around us as in us, in accordance with the myth and delusion of its sinlessness on the other..

It is after such works that modern culturology strives for, in which mythology, religion, and science coexist in a hermeneutic triad, because man at no time, regardless of ideology and system, gave up the myth, especially the ancient myths of love and supremacy, so deeply rooted in the supernatural gestures and in the internal forms of primordial words that man has never given up the rhetoric of religion, in the sense that no matter how much he fears the verity of myths, the prophecy of which has no escape in any space-time, he always finds a way out in the prophetic texts from the Genesis to the Acts of the Apostles and John's Revelation, and more importantly, finds an answer in the sciences... from those who deal exclusively with man, with his everything, soul and body, wraiths and organs, and with all his sides, light and dark..., all the way to those who deal with space and time, the humanization of space-time, and the dehumanization of man and reality, and of their understanding, which, no matter how far and wide they occupy us, bring us back to the ancient shells, wraps, covers and structures of the primordial human urge to 'art with matter', and bring us not so much to the way as to a detour.

After all, culturology - that offspring of modern philology – which, with a dose of arrogance models the structure of artistic creation, which, however projected and/or transformed into space, will always be called "text", not only when it spreads as an "ideal" sequence in time or as a functional reflection of a detailed reality branched into the human mind, but also when it comes down to only the (sub)connection (and even down to the axis part - whole, "intima" - body, clothing - subconnection) of a timeless statement, or on any structure that transforms and overflows from one imperceptible resemblance (in form, i.e. shape) to another, until it is poured out, transposed, into another matter or environment - finds impeccable material for its trinity hermeneutics in Stemarcus' "Letters of Heresy". And all heretics are similar to each other. If in nothing else, at least in the fire, in which, without a doubt, they should burn, according to ancient beliefs engraved in records, of course, they themselves should be metamorphosed, without a doubt, into a more perfect matter.

To be so absent and so present in text, in language, in reality, through mythology, through religion, through science, through the perfect structure in which everything merges and separates, means to be either a cyberneticist in the infinitely projected fields (sets) of space and time, or a semiotician in a series of letters (texts with messages not-self-found in space-time) that symbolically follow each other after the metaphor of the one-and-the-other in us, who oppose diary entries according to pure thought in the moment of revelation, and which are revealed as the end of all wanderings not so much through spiritual sacrals as through profanely dirty places, according to the logic of the topology of space, but that also means to be a scientist-philosopher, not according to the models of society as a system, but according to madness in oneself, a scientist-designer who has all the theories of systems and chaos in an art laboratory.

And all that in a novel with a flawless structure. We would say, it borrowed from the perfection and/or the mysticism of the omnipresent hexagon of the geometry of the divine providence, at which angles the forms of love intersect, overflow and transform, through the sieve of modern living, in the sense that life is a journey through forms of love. And would you fulfill the form, or would you fulfill it?! As if you are between heaven and hell, or between some of the circles between ice and fire.

Hence, the coldness or warmth of the modern way, not so much of living, but of naked being or physical existence exhausted by the innumerable madnesses of the ostensible reality, finds its consistent metaphor, which grows into an allegory of time in the latest manuscript, Stemarcus' novel "Letters of Heresy".

"Letters of Heresy" is a novel that corresponds to the

exemplary allegories of timeless literature, written in contemporary language that communicates with the modern reader, which means that neither slang nor jargon, regardless of their provenance, are foreign to it, and neither ancient nor scholastic thought are a burden to it. On the contrary, they function in a perfect harmony that corresponds to the key, paradoxically, but possible, imaginary realities in the novel - the six bronze sculptures that would be dedicated to the six types of love, which appear in the novel as titles to individual chapters: Eros, Ludus, Storge, Pragma, Mania and Agape.

The action in the novel moves through the process of creating each of the sculptures, which in itself points to semiotic multimedia works based on a literal transcription of other visual arts, but also to cybernetic observations of other sciences dealing with textual structures named texts; thus, the plasticity of sculptural modeling is anthropomorphized in language modeling, in the subordination of words that perfectly reflect the human in the sculpture and the sculptural in man, while the precision of the artistic endeavor corresponds to the scientific one.

The novel basically depicts the social life of the protagonist in an environment that does not provide a decent existence, and who reaches out to crime because of crime, according to the principle of art for art's sake because of the criminal not so much in himself as in others, because of the artistic as in us so in others, for the sake of empathy in conditions where the destruction of others is the only way up the socio-economic ladder.

"Letters of Heresy: Uncovering the Skies

Shining in Red" is a multi-layered novel in which fiction and reality, the inner and the outer in man, the hallucinatory and the inspiring, are mixed between ignorance and knowledge, and the human and the angelic devil move between the earthly and the sublime. The letters-endings of this prose give dynamism to the narrative, just as diary entries sometimes relax the accelerated course of events, illustrated by the condensed, information-filled sentences.

The author is a master of the concise and branched simple sentence, which is the result of various transpositions of the relationship between the topic and comment in the expression, as a reflection of the structural overflows of works of art that are an obsessive theme in the novel. The overflow of artistic structures is essentially illustrated by linguistic overflows achieved with complex words - authorial neologisms.

No matter how much you humble yourself in the depths of human existence and how much you rise in the unattainable endless realms of human delusion, "Letters..." is not a novel outside of reality. In that sense, the relationship between the individual and the system is leveled with a subtle note of the crime stories that fill this novel.

In other words, the philosophy of art, however, obeys the philosophy of life. But it can also be an introduction to infinite - epistolary - structures, to which, no matter how far we go, more and more paradoxically yet truly, we approach them, or rather, they approach us, in the novel "Letters of Heresy" by Stemarcus.

Dimitar Pandev

Stemarcus was born in Gevgelija (Dec 01, 1990), where he completed primary and secondary education. He graduated both at the Department of Comparative Literature and the Institute of Philosophy and also obtained a Master's degree in Screenwriting at the State University "Ss Cyril and Methodius" in Skopje, N. Macedonia.

He has won domestic and foreign literary awards for his novels, short stories and poetry and has been included in numerous anthologies. Some of his works have been published in many languages.

As of 2020, Stemarcus is an author of books of distinct genres and literary forms:

1. One way – novel (2009)
2. Apeiron – a poetry book (2010)
3. On Some Memories from a Someday Past – a poetry book (2010)
4. Hierarchical Evolution of Consciousness – analytical book on consciousness and theory of mind (2012)
5. Meta(de)construction and General Philosophy – epistemological study on the human reasoning (2012)
6. Happiness is a Verb – a book of combined spiritual, philosophical and psychological approach towards the study of human happiness (2013)
7. The Wind-and-Fog Seller and Other Stories – a short story collection (2015)

8. In Nomine – poetry book (2016)
9. Grey Shine the Universes – poetry book (2016)
10. Death Flies In Smiling – a short story collection (2017)
11. Following the White Griffin's Path - poetry book (2018)
12. Letters of Heresy - novel (2018)
13. Hypergod - poetry book (2019)
14. The Potentials of the Crime-Drama Genre Through the Feature Film Script *My name is Freedom* – screen-writing theory, master thesis (2019)
15. The Mirror Masters – theatre play (2019)

Stemarcus is a member of the Association of Writers of Macedonia, the Macedonian center of the International Theatre Institute, the European poetry platform "Versopolis" and other associations.

@stemarcus; @stemarcusbooks

CONTENTS

Endnotes

---

[1] Ouroboros - A serpent eating its tail

[2] New Testament, Acts 2:30-31

[3] Book of Revelation 10:1-3

[4] Revelation, 4

www.ingramcontent.com/pod-product-compliance
Lightning Source LLC
Chambersburg PA
CBHW031046160726
47991CB00005B/2039